EVEN THE SCORE

a Tall, Dark, and Texan novel

KATE
MEADER

Entangled Publishing, LLC
2614 South Timberline Road
Suite 109
Fort Collins, CO 80525
Visit our website at www.entangledpublishing.com.

Brazen is an imprint of Entangled Publishing, LLC. For more information on our titles, visit www.brazenbooks.com.

Edited by Liz Pelletier
Cover design by Heather Howland
Cover art from iStock

Manufactured in the United States of America

First Edition July 2015

Chapter One

Peering at her skanky reflection in the tiny mirror of the tiny dressing room at the Bella Sera Playhouse, Tess McKenzie arrived at the only possible conclusion:

The universe hates me.

The lace peekaboo neckline, aided and abetted by a faux corseted waist, left so little to the imagination she risked a wardrobe malfunction before the night was through. Over her ass, frilly tulle layers revealed a provocative band of bare thigh above black stockings.

"Five minutes to places, people."

Shit. The stage manager's sharp call lit a fire under her. With a last minute adjustment to the pink ribbon-trimmed garter, she straightened to a wobbly stand. Heels were so not her thing, especially five-inch stilettos, but creepy Derek, their esteemed director, insisted she wear them. *Can't be a French maid without the fuck-me shoes*, he'd added with a leer.

What a fine use of her—

"What a fine use of my theater degree," Amy chimed in—friend, co-worker, and brain twin. In the month since Tess had joined the cast of Chicago's premier murder mystery dinner theater show, *A Taste for Murder,* they had repeated this refrain before every performance. It might have started out as a joke, but as time went on, it felt more and more like the gods were playing a cruel prank on them. For classically trained actors, dinner theater was the equivalent of Gordon Ramsay slumming at Arby's.

That's okay. You weren't using your soul anyway.

Nudging Tess aside, Amy adjusted the beechwood rosary around her neck. It made a startling contrast against the full nun's habit blanketing her from head to toe.

Tess sighed heavily and pulled down the strip of material masquerading as a skirt. "At least you're not showing enough skin to make a career on the pole look like a viable alternative to acting."

Amy gave a sympathetic smirk. Bitch knew she'd lucked out. "In some cultures the words for actress and stripper are one and the same." She bared her teeth and used her forefinger to wipe away a smudge of Sister Mary Margaret's scarlet lipstick. It was that kind of show. "Or maybe it's actress and hooker?"

Clenching her eyes shut, Tess punched the negatives into submission and dialed up her happy. She was employed in her chosen profession, playing Claudette, the saucy French maid with more shocking secrets than she could shake her feather duster at. Five days a week and twice on Saturdays, she strutted across the boards with a flirtatious dose of *ooh la la* while old dudes and teenage boys ogled her ass.

"Remind me why I'm here again, Ames," she gritted out.

"Because the money is half decent, and it takes you one step closer to the dream, babe."

The dream. A theater storefront where Tess, Amy, and their talented but poverty-stricken actor crew could work on the projects of their hearts. Since earning their expensive degrees from Northwestern, they'd experimented with life. Some had moved to New York and L.A. Some were playing the late-night improv circuit while flirting with management jobs at Starbucks. Some had given up.

Tempted to pack it in, she had stayed the course fueled by Gran's cheerleading. The woman, more of a mother to Tess than her own, had been a ball of sunshine to the end even while her body slipped further into oblivion. Fucking cancer.

Oh, Gran, I miss you so much.

After a ten-month hiatus taking care of her grandmother in Terra Haute, Indiana, Tess had returned to Chicago and found her core posse still here, living on ramen and crazy ambition. As soon as they made enough to fund their theater's first year, they were going to grab their dreams by the balls.

And speaking of nuts… The door to the dressing room was thrown open, and in strode Director Derek and his scene-stealing leather pants.

"Where's Millie?" he snapped while his lascivious gaze ate up Tess with a slimy spoon. Instinctively, she stepped back. Derek had a flasher-in-a-raincoat proclivity for brushing those leathers against her hips while trying to engage her 34Cs in deep conversation.

Millie blew out of the bathroom, pulling up the triple

strength support hose that was part of her costume as the Countess Radwanska, an aging Polish noble who has a pretty strong motive for bumping off her husband.

"Did you knock, Derek?" Millie grabbed her elegant cigarette holder. "Or did you waltz in, hoping to catch an exposed nipple or something a little juicier?"

Visibly affronted, Derek flushed an ugly shade of red. "Not sure what you're implying, Millie, but—"

"Just that you're a perv, Der."

In sisterly solidarity, all three of them glared at Derek until he backed up under the weight of their collective disapproval.

"Chop, chop, ladies," he sputtered, underlining his shaky authority with a clap of his undoubtedly sweaty hands. "We've got a full house tonight, so go sell some booze."

Tess tamped down a budding growl. The worst part about this gig was the actors—the freaking talent—had to serve the audience while staying in character before the official showtime. Slinging cardboard chicken and soggy fettuccine to tourists was yep, a fine use of her theater degree. But the tips were good, especially for the French maid who twitched her tail and turned the accent up to *onze*.

"What's that again about the words for actress and stripper being the same in some cultures?" she asked Amy, who was tying her rosary beads around her waist, trying to give the sack she was wearing a shape.

"Actress and hooker, babe."

Tess shook her head. Another day, another piece of her soul down the drain.

"*'Allo, mes amis*, what can I get you this eve-*ven*-ing?"

The response? A tableful of blank stares from a family of five — mom, dad, and three surly teens.

She tried again. "Zee wine, zee cocktails, zee Perrier?"

Tourist Dad's jaw practically grazed the hardwood floor, but his eyes stayed locked on her corset-enhanced rack. *That's right, bud, they're breasts and your wife has a pair.*

"George!" the woman beside him snapped. She nailed Tess with a keep-your-mitts-off-my-husband glare. *As if, lady.*

"The Robert Mondavi Pinot Noir," Tourist Wifey said primly, lifting her sharp gaze from the skeletal wine list. Two reds, two whites, and a rosé for the truly adventurous. "Is that any good?"

"Zee best of Napa." And at the outrageous fifty dollars a pop the Bella Sera playhouse was charging, at least a ten dollar tip right there if these guys didn't stiff her at the end of the night.

Awesome sauce. She was now measuring her worth in Robert Mondavi jug wine.

Order taken and smile pinned on, she turned quickly.

Too quickly.

On her deadly spindles, she tottered and felt the slippery hardwood give from under her. The room tilted. Like something out of a French farce — oh, the irony — she fought to keep her ass from making a painful meet-cute with the floor.

Going, going…

But just as her right heel missed finding purchase, two strong hands, tucked beneath her elbows, broke her fall.

"Careful now, honey," she heard in a whiskey-rough drawl.

A flicker of recognition pinged her chest just as warm, callused palms righted her balance and turned her deftly toward her savior.

It couldn't be. Not here. Not now.

Even with the added height, which gave her five-four frame a solid boost, she still had to look up. Into the darkest midnight eyes she had ever seen.

She knew those eyes.

She knew that jaw.

And by the looks of that grim slash of a mouth, he knew who she was, and worse, he remembered exactly what she had done to him.

Thank you, universe. You're the best.

"Well, if it ain't Miss Weddin' Wrecker herself," Hunter Dade said, still with a country twang, backed up by a Texan oil field's worth of heat.

The man who had vowed to put her over his knee the next time he saw her was back— And he was as ticked off as ever.

Sixty seconds.

He'd had sixty seconds of heaven from door to catch before he realized his mistake.

To think that the sugar sweet ass Hunter was admiring as he made strides to his table belonged to Tess McKenzie. Covered in frilly layers, she'd been leaning forward just enough to give a tantalizing glimpse of smooth, peachy skin above her sexy stockings. In those heels, damn, her legs were so killer he was already imagining the myriad ways he would get those stockings off.

Fast, fast, and faster.

Zeroing in on her ass, his pulse had quickened when the best thing imaginable happened: the honey fell right into his arms. Unfortunately, this particular sweetness came laced with strychnine.

Tess was the menace responsible for the worst day of his life. Her interference a year ago had cost him a deal, a wife, and a hundred and fifty thousand dollars in vendor fees for the wedding that never happened.

"Hey…" she said, uncertainty in her voice. That'd be a first. The woman was a snob, an artsy free spirit who hated his roughneck ass from the moment she laid eyes on him after one of her theatrical efforts. His then-fiancée and Tess had been college roommates, and Hunter knew it was important to his future wife that he make an effort.

Making an effort was one thing; lying his balls off was another. So he didn't know dick about "the Arts" and his ignorance showed like a nasty rash on his skin. He might have commented that Tess's show was a particularly special brand of bullshit. Some crap about women in ancient Greece punishing their men by withholding sex. It had hit all his buttons, and he had no problem speaking his mind. Neither did Tess and they'd— Well, they'd gotten into it good.

That argument had been the most fun he'd had all year.

Back in the present, his hands still cupped her smooth, silky elbows. He needed to release her.

Every day as a partner in Score Property, one of the fastest-growing real estate development companies in the U.S., he made whip-fast decisions, yet now he had a crystal clear choice before him, and he couldn't think for shit. That enticing freckle on her left breast, an alarmingly half-exposed left breast, was fogging his brain to mush. What would it taste like, that freckle?

Nothing. Freckles don't taste of anything, but the scent invading his nostrils told him this woman's skin would taste so fine. Dangerous, not-coming-back-from-it fine.

His hold had drawn her into the cage of his body, leaving her no choice but to palm his chest right over his nipple. The one that was hardening with each passing second. The touch of her slender hand was light, but not so much it wouldn't hold its own fisting and stroking and working his—how in the hell had his brain gone there?

He let go.

Pausing as he ran the play in his head was a mistake. It signified weakness, and she stepped right into the gap, wresting back any advantage he had in surprising her.

"So how've you been, cowboy?"

"Just fine, princess."

He kept his response flat, giving nothing away. If she looked down, she might have noticed his emotion was distilled to his uncomfortably tight jeans. What the fuck was happening here? So it had been a while since he'd released his pent-up energy inside a woman, but this was Tess McKenzie. They despised each other. The last time they'd been this close, he had been losing his ever-loving shit on her, a memory he conjured with ease and not a small amount of embarrassment.

More than a little pissed by his body's reaction to her, he aimed for the jugular. "Still playin' at your hobby then?"

Jackpot. Two spots of color lit high on her cheeks. For someone with such a fancy education and acting pedigree, this dinner theater gig didn't seem up to her usual standards.

"It pays the bills," she said, a proud jut to her chin that, along with the widening of those beautiful green eyes, was the only signal she was affected by his mockery. *Aw, shit.* The answering lurch in his chest felt like pettiness.

"I should…" She gestured with raised eyebrows that she needed to get back to it. Fine with him, they were all caught up. With his eyes locked on hers, he stepped aside, giving her more than enough room to thread her smoking body through as she walked past. Still with that chin and nose high in the air. The woman had spirit. He'd give her that.

A few more steps and he had found his party. He slumped to his chair, one of four seated around a cabaret style table about twenty feet from the stage. Flynn Cross, his business partner, drinking buddy, and the guy he could rely on for a pickup game at two in the morning, eyed him with interest.

"Is that…?"

"Yep."

The clip to Hunter's tone should have been enough to shut it down, but "leave well alone" and "personal space" were not part of Flynn's vocabulary.

"Well, I'll be." He squinted in what Hunter assumed was Tess's direction. "She looks hot. Wonder if she does private shows in that costume."

"Are you ogling the talent again, hon?"

The stunning blonde to Flynn's left ran a finger along his jaw and turned it to face her. Flynn broke into the shit-eating grin he had been wearing since she agreed to become Mrs. Cross six months back. They were here seeing this junk that passed for entertainment because Flynn wanted to take Becca out to do something touristy for her visit to Chicago.

She was completing her OB/GYN residency at Baylor but planned to move here to set up house with Flynn when she finished in eight months.

Flynn kissed her softly. "I only have eyes for you, Becs. I was thinking about my boy's needs."

Becca curved her skeptical gaze around Flynn to take in Hunter. "Handsome, wealthy, and Texan is its own calling card. You don't need my man's help."

Hunter tipped an imaginary hat. "No, ma'am, I don't."

"And polite, too." Her assessing gaze turned soft with compassion he neither wanted nor needed. If he had a dime for every well-meaning look he'd received in the last year, he'd have a motherfucking load of dimes. "The right girl's just around the corner, Hunter."

"Or how about the *wrong* girl at the other end of the bar?" Flynn gave an unsubtle chin jerk in the direction Hunter was no longer looking. There could be a five-alarm fire happening over there, and he'd be ignoring it.

Becca wasn't ignoring it, but as she had seen Tess only once before, Hunter felt safe the interfering maid of honor would pass without comment. On his wedding day, Tess had looked positively demure in a jade gown that set off to perfection her auburn hair and those eyes the shade of melted shamrocks. "Demure" and "Tess" weren't even in the same zip code tonight.

"We can do better than *that* for Hunter," Becca said dismissively as she perused the playbill for the show. "I know just the girl. Vassar, Rotary Club, child psychologist. She's the complete package."

Right. So was Jenna, his former fiancée. A bluestocking Chicago socialite, a charity doyenne, perfect on paper. These days, Hunter was done with overeducated, careerless, rich girls who liked to play tourist with guys from the wrong side of the Mason-Dixon line.

Flynn leaned in and whispered, "Is this the first time you've seen her since the day she got all up in your business?"

Hunter nodded, not trusting himself to speak. After so long, his fury at her should have faded. He never lost control, not since he'd been a punk-ass teen. But that day—his wedding day—raw emotion had done a number on his granite tight grip, and he'd gone apeshit on Tess. Strange, when the woman he should have been blaming was the beautiful bride who had elected to jilt him at the altar in a church filled with four hundred guests. But getting mad at Jenna was impossible. She was so pure and innocent that the sight of her with tears streaming down her porcelain cheeks had melted the hot fist of anger in his chest. He had loved her wholesome regality, how she would make the textbook society wife. His reward for crawling out of the dirt of a hardscrabble upbringing in a run-down trailer park in Texas.

But all that changed in a heartbeat when the maid of honor pulled him aside ten minutes after the ceremony was supposed to begin. Snooty Princess Tess had loved being the bearer of that particular piece of news.

Thinking on that stalled his brain, so he was glad for the interruption, even if it was a guy sporting a penguin suit and a monocle, asking him what he wanted to drink. Jesus H. Christmas.

"Double Scotch," Hunter said. "Glenmorangie twelve year if you have it."

Mr. Peanut smirked. That'd be a no, then. "Will Dewar's do?"

"Sure."

"So, the maid of honor is an actress," Flynn muttered as soon as Mr. Peanut left to get the drinks in. "That's interesting."

Hunter turned to his friend and gave him the stare down. "Is it now?"

Flynn smiled, annoying as all fuck. "How's the Crandall deal shaping up?"

"I'm going down there in a week."

"Alone?"

"Yep."

Flynn cleared his throat. "Gonna be tough to close. You know what Old Man Crandall is like."

Sure did. When it came to business associates, TJ Crandall liked good family values and men already hog-tied to a woman, all of which made Hunter the odd man out. Tess's big mouth had left Hunter with a big problem.

"What's Old Man Crandall like?" Becca asked, amusement warming her voice at the moniker, which made him sound like a Scooby Doo villain.

Flynn chuckled, a little evilly. "Let's just say that if he thinks our boy here is single and on the prowl, he won't want to see him within a mouse fart's distance of the young and firm Mrs. Crandall." He cupped imaginary assets with both hands to demonstrate just how young and firm Buffy was.

With an indulgent eye roll at her man-child fiancé, Becca tilted her head in query. "Why aren't you going down instead?" A reasonable question given Crandall's preference for lovesick, henpecked idiots.

"This is Hunter's deal," Flynn said softly.

He would trust his life to Flynn Cross and the other third of their posse in Score Property, Brody Kane, but the guys knew this was personal for him. That land TJ was selling meant more than a multi-million dollar development to Hunter; it was the best way to honor the memory of his sister, Alison.

It would be his redemption.

Becca leaned across Flynn and hitched both dark blond eyebrows. "Hunter, hon, you need me to play your fake girlfriend? You know I love me some Texan man flesh."

Horror crossed Flynn's brow. Making a show of it, he pushed her back out of Hunter's sight line. "You've already got a hunk of Texan man flesh keeping you warm, sweets. You ain't playin' house with this one. I might never get you back."

Hunter plastered on a smile over his disappointment. He had planned to take Becca aside later and run that very idea by her, but Flynn's hands-off-my-woman reaction told him that wasn't up for negotiation. Even a friendship as good as theirs had its limits.

"Thanks, Becca. I'll work something out."

When it came to women, Hunter wasn't exactly hurting for attention, so finding someone to accompany him to Crandall's ranch was not the problem. The problem was the expectation that went hand in hand with a trip like that. TJ would spot a casual hook-up a mile away, and any woman by Hunter's side would have to be clear on the end game. Pretend they were in it for life, but understand there was no possible chance of it lasting beyond the weekend.

She would have to be a friend, a lesbian…or an excellent actress.

"I know you're thinking about it," Flynn said, low enough to keep Becca ignorant of the specifics.

Unavoidably, Hunter found his gaze drawn to Tess as she weaved that body built like a Coke bottle between the tight web of tables. He wasn't alone in his interest. Every set of male eyes between the ages of eight and eighty was locked on that sweet ass like it was magnetic.

Pity she was a pain in *his* ass.

"She's trouble."

"And the last time you two talked at the wedding that never happened"—Flynn emphasized *talked* and added air quotes in case Hunter was too dumb to get it—"it looked like you wanted to take your chat to the honeymoon suite at the Drake. Hell, *I* was jonesing for a cigarette after those fireworks."

"That's how people act when they despise each other," Hunter muttered. Wasn't it? He might have let the odd inappropriate thought about Tess cross his mind back then. Hot or not was pretty much uppermost in every guy's mind on meeting a woman for the first time, never mind that she was a friend of your intended. To think there was more to it— That was just crazy.

When Flynn's only response was a know-it-all eyebrow lift, Hunter shifted uncomfortably in his seat. "Cross, you're overdrawn at the memory bank."

"Whatever gets you through the night," his so-called friend said. "All I know is you never once looked at the bride the way you're looking at the maid of honor right this minute. So you had your reasons for marrying Jenna, but that was then and this is now. The Crandall deal? Think of it as killing two birds."

Killing was about right. The thought of spending a moment with Tess, never mind an entire weekend, curdled his blood, and then sent it hurtling in a torrent to his groin. When not thinking of imaginative ways to murder her, he'd be consumed with conjuring up even more imaginative ways to screw her brains out.

Fast, slow, all night long.

But Flynn might be on to something. *Killing two birds…*

Another thought formed in his brain. A shiny, brilliant thought. While he was earning his redemption with the Crandall deal, maybe he could mix in a little payback. Bring Princess Tess to her knees and make her rue the day she interfered in his life.

At the bar, she was leaning over to talk. That move hitched those sexy ruffles and flashed another sliver of gorgeous thigh, bisected by the lacy top of those stockings and…a garter belt. Damn. Pink, silky, like a forecast of the succulent heaven between her legs. He nearly groaned at the thought of those stocking tops molded to her thighs. Would the lace emboss her pale skin, creating a pattern he could smooth away with his tongue? What kind of sounds would she make as he kissed her inner thighs, first stop on the journey to true north?

So payback wouldn't exactly be a chore. Sure, she was off-limits before, but now the stoplight on his attraction to her had changed to green. Revenge was a dish best served in bed— And Tess McKenzie was about to get a five-course meal.

Chapter Two

Tess lowered her still shaking body to a chair in the dressing room and buried her face in her hands.

What a catastrophe.

Rarely did a show pass without someone flubbing a line, missing a cue, or standing downstage blocking the action, but tonight she had achieved royal states of idiocy. At the pivotal moment when Claudette was supposed to announce the tennis pro had knocked her up, the character's name fled her brain. Along with her next line. And the fact that she was supposed to beat him over the head with her feather duster, the one she had left in the closet during the open-close-doors-musical-farce-runabout (say *that* ten times fast).

Hell if she could concentrate on anything after her run-in with Hunter Dade. What in the name of all that was holy was he doing in a theater? The guy was a Philistine who hated all things artistic. Not that *A Taste of Murder* was great art, but still. The stage lights prevented clear views of the audience more than ten feet out, but she could feel his presence like a malevolent cloud.

Sneering. Judging. Hating.

Her elbows tingled where he had touched her with those sandpaper rough hands. Her skin burned from the focus of those devil blue eyes. And how could she have forgotten how tall he was or how possessively he claimed the space around her? Well-sculpted muscles had drawn taut under his shirt when her palm grazed his chest. Raw, animalistic power at her fingertips.

The man had always been an incredibly fine specimen, though his body was more likely forged in hellfire than a gym. Hunter Dade probably thought gyms were for pansies.

That grudge the size of the Lone Star state? He clearly still owned it, and while she had played the role of reluctant messenger that day because Jenna was too upset—*cough*, cowardly—to come clean in person, Tess's heart squeezed at causing someone pain. Even if that someone was a newly-minted billionaire looking to acquire a trophy wife and the attractive lakefront property her family owned. That bright September day, as he rained words down on her like blows, Tess was hard pressed to tell if he was angrier about losing a wife or losing the deal.

She suspected it was the deal.

Chicago's latest "It" couple had met at a charity event, the new meat market for outrageously wealthy singles. Soon Hunter was bringing out the big guns with expensive jewelry and lavish trips, all while grooming Jenna's father on a lucrative property development that would turn into her dowry. Jenna had always been as weak as water where her parents were concerned. When, on what was supposed to be the happiest day of her life, she had a panic attack in the vestibule of Winnetka Presbyterian ten seconds before the organist launched into Pachelbel's *Canon in D*, Tess had pulled her aside and gouged the truth out of her.

Jenna liked Hunter, but she just wasn't sure she loved him.

Four hundred exquisitely dressed sardines sat in the church pews, the flowers alone cost ten thousand dollars, but the bride only *liked* the groom. Jenna could tell the difference, because she was pretty sure she *did* love someone— Only it wasn't the Texan who had given her a diamond ring the size of his ego. She had met middle school teacher, Steve, at the animal shelter where they both volunteered, and the romance of puppy baths and poop-scooping had sucked her in deep.

Might have been easier on everyone involved if she'd come to this epiphany before Hunter made that trip down the aisle.

"You okay?" Amy squeezed Tess's shoulder, hauling her back to the unfriendly confines of the Bella Sera's dressing room. Her friend had already changed out of her nun's habit back into bar crawl comfort wear of jeans and light sweater. "You seemed a little off your game tonight."

"Think I'm coming down with something," Tess said, not in the mood for sharing.

"Looks like you need some serious ethanol therapy. Get out of those sexy threads and into a dry martini."

"Nah, think I'll skip it. I've got a date with Ben & Jerry." Thrown off-kilter by Hunter Dade, she would much rather go home and process it. Maybe in the fetal position.

"Okay," Ames murmured, concern bracketing her mouth. "I'll call you tomorrow, and you can fill me in on your fascinating love life with the man whores from Vermont."

Fifteen minutes later, alone with her misery, Tess hadn't moved a muscle except to crook her finger as she scrolled through text messages from her mother.

My therapist wants to set up a conference call. How about Tuesday?

How about, *Bite me, Mom*?

"Not your best performance tonight, Tess."

First Hunter Dade, then her mother. Now the third prong of the shit-happens-in-threes crapfest chose to rear its ugly-ass head in the form of Director Derek. He stood at the door in those ridiculous leather pants, molded so tight they had to be a threat to his sperm count.

"Sorry about that," she said with a thin smile. "Couldn't seem to get my act together."

He wore the unfocused gaze of the drunk, unsurprising as he spent most of the show tippling from a hip flask. His creepy smile sent shivers crawling along her skin.

"Maybe we should run some lines." This time, the slur in his voice was pronounced, and before she could respond, he had closed the gap between them. Those leathers sure didn't hamper his movement.

Feeling at a disadvantage in her seated position, she stood, but he moved in more quickly than she expected and curled a hand around her hip. His fingers bit into her flesh.

"Derek, it's been a long night, and I'm tired."

"Have a drink with me, and I'll drive you home," he said, placing his body flush against hers. Stinging booze fumes almost knocked her off her heels, and instinctively, she pushed back with her hand on his chest.

Ugh! His shirt was damp with sweat. Her hand had no impact on his drunken lurch, and now she recognized more than a haze of alcohol in his eyes. Against her stomach, the hard ridge of his erection jutted, putting her on notice of his dangerous arousal.

Shit.

The stillness in the air confirmed a troubling conclusion: no one else was here. The crew and actors had left for the night, and the only noises were the trip-hammer of thoughts knocking around her skull and Derek's serrated breathing. Rising panic clawed like razor blades at her insides.

"Got to go, Der," she said amiably, working to keep the shake from her voice. Getting snippy might provoke him further. Hired less than a month ago on Amy's rec, she barely knew him, and though he'd always come across as harmless, she had no real clue what he was capable of.

His lightened grip on her waist forced air out of her lungs in relief, but she had exhaled too soon. He slithered his palm to the small of her back and pressed her toward him, a move that ushered in reality once more.

"Tess, I've been fantasizing about sucking your spectacular tits for weeks." He inclined his head to the valley between said tits, forcing her to recoil and move out of the reach of his slack, spittle-flecked mouth. "I think we should get to know each other better."

Images pulsed through her brain, a patchwork memory she had locked down to a deep corner of her mind. Another set of grasping hands, a similarly fleshy mouth. She had escaped then, and no way would this asshole get the better of her now. Adrenaline fueled her veins, pumping up her fight response.

"Let. Me. Go."

A thunderstorm brewed in his eyes. "Come on, Tess, why

you wanna be a stuck-up bitch?"

Oh, he had no idea. She toed up like a Pamplona bull, raised a knee, and then she stomped the prick's foot with the heels he was so fond of. His howl, a satisfyingly girlish sound, was the most entertaining thing out of his mouth in the entire time she had worked for him.

"Consider that my notice, asshole. I quit." She thrust out her hand. "Now, give me your car keys."

"*Whaaah?*" Derek moaned, hopping up and down.

"You're not driving in that condition." As for how the scumbag got home, she didn't give two shits. She just knew she couldn't live with herself if he put anyone in danger. "If you don't hand over those keys, my next kick will be so hard you'll have three Adam's apples!"

Derek's whiskey-clouded eyes cleared for a split-second sneer, but when she fisted his sweat-damp shirt, he handed the keys over without a word. Her clothes and backpack hung on a rail, and she lurched over to it in her weaponized heels, amazed she had strength to walk. The moment was fast catching up to her.

Her boss had made a pass at her.

She'd assaulted him and quit her job.

Holy fuck.

"I'm not paying you out, Tess," Derek whined. "No tips, no salary, nothing."

"Whatever, I have your car, d-bag," she threw back over her shoulder, all tough girl bravado. Heart in chaos and body in a daze, she punished the floor with her heels, desperate for the safety of the cool Chicago night. Several taut moments later, bone-shaking fear in her veins that Derek might follow, she pushed through the door that led to the front of the house and slammed into a wall.

A mountainous, inflexible, hot-blooded wall.

"'Bout time you showed your face, princess."

For the second time that night, Tess looked into the wild navy eyes of the man who despised her. Straight-up handsomeness had passed Hunter Dade by. There had always been something too stark, too hungry about him. Bootblack hair, more closely cropped than she remembered, added to the image of a six-four tower of lean, mean badassery.

He had changed. Compared to a year ago, everything about him now was…more. More harsh, more raw, more potent. With his unabashed masculinity, he'd make a perfect Stanley in *Streetcar*.

His hands had reached out to steady her and landed on her hips. Yet again, she was locked in his solid embrace, and what was more shocking? She liked it. Craved it. Warmth rivaling a furnace flooded her skin. After being manhandled by Derek, she should have felt skittish about another man's touch, especially at the spot where the jerk's clammy hand must have left some sweaty residue. Hunter's hand felt light but pleasantly unyielding.

"I…" She threw a not-so-furtive glance over her shoulder, only to spy Derek at the end of the corridor. On seeing her—on seeing Hunter—the weasel-faced crapmonkey bolted in the other direction. Five seconds later, the alley door exit sounded a petulant bang.

"I… I have to leave."

Hunter gathered her close in an almost protective sweep and looked over her head, then back at her with an unfathomable gaze. For a moment, she forgot how to breathe.

"Who was that?"

"My director." She blinked. "Ex-director." Pushing Hunter aside, which was as difficult as it sounded, she dumped her backpack and clothes on a stool and stepped behind the bar. The best scotch on offer was Dewar's. She poured a double.

"What happened back there?" Hunter growled.

She knocked the whiskey back in one gulp, its warm burn shaking loose her dazed senses. With a punctuating slam of the glass down on the bar, she gave a mental hitch of her bootstraps and strutted back out to the front of the house, renewed purpose in her demeanor. "Nothing, all under control."

She needed to get back on speaking terms with reality, namely why Hunter Dade was here. Because, if she knew one thing, it was the man was not her biggest fan. With hands fisted at her hips, she took a sharp breath to fuel what she said next. "Okay, I'll give you two minutes, Tex. I won't even talk back, just let you get it all out."

Whoa, listen to her, kicking zee ass and taking zee names.

He threaded his arms and delivered that gunfighter squint they probably teach in Texas preschools. "But you talkin' back is half the fun, princess. Besides, I'm not sure I wanna get on your wrong side right now. You look like you could slice through a log with those eyes."

A whiplash of emotions pummeled her as the enormity of tonight's events doubled back around the block and hit her square in the solar plexus.

"I— I just quit my job." That wasn't the worst thing to have happened, but she'd need time to work up to the bigger stuff. Tears—*of fury*, she insisted—pricked the backs of her eyelids.

"Hey, now." In a split second, he was there, running a thumb along her cheek, over her jawline, and finishing with a swipe of the tear that had finally made good on its threat to fall. His palm unfurled to cup her neck, an incredibly sensual move that coiled warm, feminine pleasure in her belly. Sure didn't hurt that he happened to smell incredible.

Those dark eyes searched her face. "Did somebody…" He sent an ice pick of a look toward backstage. "Tess, did that guy hurt you?"

"No—no. Just creative differences." She shook her head, still held in Hunter's big hand, and the slight friction of his callused palm against her jaw made her light-headed. A shiver coursed through her vitals. She felt both protected and unbearably aroused.

It must have been the darkened bar. Or the adrenaline. Or the fact that she hadn't gotten any in foh-evah.

The air *snap-crackle-popped* between them. Hunter's eyes stayed trained on hers like he was seeking to get inside her head—or penetrate every defense she had spent the last ten years fortifying. A brief image of him thrusting into her, deep and to the root, slammed a bolt of desire so potent through her that she almost splayed a hand on his immense chest for balance.

Get it together. Knowing if she touched him, a case of severe grope-itis would inevitably follow, she took a shaky step back out of his reach and a deep breath with it. He watched her with those midnight eyes.

"So, you're out of a job. You got somethin' else lined up?"

She could go back to waiting tables at the Hard Rock or walking dogs for that crazy lady in Lincoln Park, but her theater dream was starting to look more and more distant. Fucking Derek and his fucking leather pants.

"I'll find something."

"I've no doubt you will. You're a great actress."

Shocked laughter spilled from her lips. She could do with some cheering up.

"This from the guy who thought *Lysistrata* was an abomination, and anyone who performed in it was an idiot."

"Just 'cause I didn't agree with the politics of that piece of shit play doesn't mean I didn't think you were any good in it. I mean, the plot had women not puttin' out so their men wouldn't go to war." He gave a melancholy headshake, clearly still disturbed by Aristophanes's classic about gender relations.

"I know it's tough to wrap your *Y* chromosomes around the concept of female empowerment."

"I've got no problem with female empowerment, but everyone knows you catch more flies with honey than vinegar." He rubbed his stubble-rough jaw and fixed her with a penetrating gaze. "You just don't like when people disagree with you, Tess."

Thrown off guard by the deepness of his tone—and okay, that very attractive five o'clock shadow—she went on the offensive, her default position with him. "I don't like when people talk on topics they don't know the first thing about."

"So I can't have an opinion?"

"Not if you're expressing it purely to be pigheaded."

A wolfish smile played on his lips. "You're so stubborn you could float upstream."

"So are you." *Excellent comeback, Tess. Those improv classes were worth every dime.*

His wicked grin stretched wider and made her skin tingle. Other parts, too.

That he was still annoying as all get out was not in question, but how come she liked him better this time around? The Dewar's must have gone straight to her addled brain.

"So this job…" He lazily surveyed the bar and stage, finishing with a thorough assessment of Tess in all her French maid glory. "Or this former job doesn't seem like your usual, Tess. Sure you were funny as fuck up there, but it makes me curious."

Something lurched in her chest at his compliment, this weird vibe swirling around them. An odd compulsion to justify her choice to take on this gig gripped her. "I need to raise money for a theater company I'm trying to get off the ground. Acting jobs that pay well are hard to come by, so that's why I was shaking zee derrière."

That seemed to throw him, if throwing Hunter Dade was possible. She couldn't readily interpret the emotions scrawled across his face, but she'd hazard a guess good thoughts were not rising to the top.

As much as Tess hated being the messenger that fateful day, she had done it for her friend—and curiously enough for Hunter, though he would probably never acknowledge the favor. Now, waiting for his hammer to fall was making every cell burn.

"I wish you'd just do it," she muttered.

His spicy scent was already scrambling her brain; his intoxicating proximity wreaked havoc on whatever hormones had not already raised the white flag. Incrementally, he moved in, close enough that she could see a silver ring around his darkening irises. The motion claimed her personal space and forced her ass into an acquaintance with a barstool.

"Do what?"

"You know." Scold her, punish her, kiss her. God, that's what she wanted—needed—this very moment. Her legs parted ever so slightly, traitorously inviting him into their embrace. *Oh, Claudette, you French hussy.*

"Plenty of time for us to get into it good, princess," he drawled. "You drivin'?"

Flustered by her body's overheated response to him, she shook her head. Closed those legs. "I don't have a car. I usually take the train."

"Not tonight, Tess. You're with me."

Chapter Three

While Tess changed in her bedroom, Hunter took a good look around the tastefully furnished duplex in Chicago's Gold Coast, a wealthy enclave on the city's Near North Side, and gave a low whistle. Four million. At least. His own was worth four-five, but then he'd paid top dollar 'cause it was lakefront.

The art on the walls was the real deal, too. He didn't know much, but he knew that. Gilt frames, touchable paint, the whole nine. Tess McKenzie was doing okay for herself, so why she was shaking her ass to raise money for this theater of hers was a mystery.

But then everything about her was a contradiction.

Hunter wasn't given to great displays of emotion, but hell if Tess didn't rev his engine. Something had happened with Leather Nuts backstage, something that had spooked her and made her quit—and the fact she wouldn't tell him about it infuriated him. There was nothing Hunter hated more than a man treating a woman with disrespect whether it was with words, unwanted hands, or fists. His sister had fallen victim to a nut job who thought he could use her as his plaything. No way was Hunter going to put up with that if it was in his power to stop it.

For a brief moment in that bar, Tess had looked so exposed, her face soft with emotion. Soft under his touch, too. But two clicks later, the princess was back from her vulnerability timeout with nose raised high like she'd just tripped over an open sewer line.

Clearly, she still thought Hunter was an uncultured jerk who led with his wallet and his ego. A redneck, a Texas hick. She had never said those things to his face, but he knew exactly how this society girl's mind worked. If presented with Hunter on one side and a sweating, nostril-flaring bull on the other, she'd struggle to pick the human out of the lineup. And for some reason not yet clear, he cared about how she saw him.

As for how he saw her…

Tess emerged into the living room, having changed into a pair of exercise pants whose primary function was to give a guy's dick a workout, along with a tank top that read "Obsessive Cupcake Disorder." Cute. And sexy. With each new viewing, she aroused him more.

Set in a messy knot, her auburn hair was a sight to behold and sent his mind tripping over the possibilities. That gorgeous crown would look so good fanned against his pillow while he lowered his body over hers. Once he'd had his fill of her that way, he'd turn her over and bury his fingers in her hair for leverage. Enter her slow until he was balls deep. She was so goddamn petite he bet she'd fit snugger than a rubber around his cock.

Her eyebrows arched at the sight on the coffee table.

"Please. Make yourself at home."

He'd brought out a tub of Ben & Jerry's from the kitchen and embedded a couple of spoons in the creamy depths. Best way to start a tricky conversation off right.

"You ready to tell me what happened back at the theater?"

Discomfort brushed across her pretty features, but she dialed up a smooth slate foxy fast. "You ready to get this show on the road and tear me a new one?"

"Not one for the small talk, huh? And so, so sure I'm gonna shout at you."

She crossed her arms over those beautiful breasts. "Hmm, there's the little matter of what went down between us the last time we met. How—"

"You destroyed my wedding day?"

She nodded, eyes wide with anticipation. This woman wasn't worried about getting her ass chewed out. She wanted it. Wanted to get into it just as much as he did. Well, wasn't that interesting? Except now he wasn't mad at her for the reasons she thought. His blood was boiling for a whole host of other reasons.

He wanted to fight, and then he wanted to fuck.

What the hell is wrong with me?

This was headed for dangerous territory. He needed to put a tether on his emotions because if she got him this stirred up after just a few minutes, how the hell was he going to feel spending a weekend with her, pretending she was his?

His. Christ, that word was enough to tighten every inch of him with cell-deep want.

She sighed her annoyance that he refused to play her game. "I invited you in, Hunter, because you insisted on driving me home and then gave me the silent treatment on the way. I could just as easily have taken the train."

He shut his eyes, just long enough for a movie of a Tess-induced train riot to screen on the backs of his eyelids. Fists flying, teeth broken, friendships destroyed as men vied to get closer to her lush body barely covered in that incendiary French maid outfit.

And now he was turning hard again.

Flynn's words echoed like a spectral taunt. *You never once looked at Jenna the way you're looking at the maid of honor right now.*

Man, he hated that Flynn was right. In Hunter's world, there were two kinds of women: the vow-takin', cookie-bakin', baby-makin' kind, and the ones you wanted to lose your mind and dick in. Until tonight, he would have put Tess in the first category with Jenna. There had been a mild attraction to his former fiancée, but it was her potential as the perfect wife that drew him to her. Hitting his thirties, Hunter was at that point where it was time to start putting down roots instead of putting it to anything in a skirt. And if his money could open the door to a better quality woman, he was happy to use it. He was under no illusion that he and Jenna had a great passion, but they were a good match.

Then along came uppity Tess, ruining all those best laid plans. It was good to be reminded of it.

Willing his cock to behave, he drew a fighting breath, lowered himself to the sofa, and patted the spot beside him. "Have a seat, princess."

Hunter Dade sat in Stepfather Number Two's living room, no doubt sizing up Tess's net worth and concluding she was a spoiled society girl. Those princess jibes said it all. In his mind, she was the snooty-nosed, rich-bitch busybody who told her friend marrying this Texas bruiser would be a huge-ass mistake. Well, Tess was right on that score. But she had excellent reasons, and now that he was here, she was going to let it all out.

Warrior Tess, activate.

Ready to rumble, she crossed her arms and sat at the opposite end of the sofa, steeling her body for the battle ahead. But then came her first mistake: her gaze snagged on that big meaty palm of his as it lay splayed on the cushion. He could use it to spread her thighs wide and rub the callused heel roughly against her sensitive flesh—

Oh, mercy me.

She had invited the beast over the threshold, but now she was uncertain if she relished the fight. Apparently, though, her body was completely on board with the idea of the horizontal mambo.

"Hunter—"

The opening bars of "Ding Dong The Witch is Dead" filled the room with its tinny dirge. She reached over to where her phone lay on the coffee table and hit the decline button.

"Interesting ringtone," he murmured.

"My mother," she said without thinking. Shit. "It's complicated."

"Sounds like it." The flicker of understanding in those sharp eyes surprised her. A ringtone like that could be so easily misconstrued, and while Tess might think two-time Oscar winner and national treasure, Deborah Patton—aka "Mom"—would give the Wicked Witch of the West a run for her money, she didn't actually wish for her demise.

Not all the time, anyway.

"Hunter," she restarted. "About that day—"

"That's not why I'm here."

It wasn't? "I… I thought you'd want to talk about it."

He speared her from beneath hooded lids. "Why the fuck would I want to talk about it? The only person I wanted to talk to was my bride, but instead of lettin' a man and a woman sort out their problems, you appointed yourself judge, jury, and executioner of my marriage." He leaned back on the sofa, the casual pose doing little to disguise the seething muscles rippling beneath his button-down. "I'm not one for rehashin' things, Tess. What's done is done."

Shock numbed her throat. She struggled to push the words out. "Just like that?"

"Just like that." A spark of passion in his eyes contrasted with the grim set of his mouth. "Now, how're your feet?"

"My what?"

"They must be sore after a long night in those cages. Hand 'em over."

She couldn't have heard that right. "That's it? What's done is done, now hand over your feet?"

"Tess, I've moved on. And as for Jenna"—he rubbed his mouth—"well, I hear she's with someone else now."

Sadness colored his voice. Did he have the faintest idea that his former fiancée had been cheating on him? From that hurt tone on saying Jenna's name, Tess guessed not.

She had assumed Hunter was marrying Jenna for her massive dowry and the upward mobility it would give him in his bid for world domination, but maybe she had it wrong. Maybe Hunter had been crazy in love with her friend.

That pinched. She didn't like that it did, nor did she like that she didn't like it.

His sense of loss seemed to fill the space between them. She wanted to hug away his pain. Maybe smooth it away with her greedy hands and greedier kisses…

Okaaay, ice cream was needed. Stat.

Her gaze dipped to the Ben & Jerry's Phish Food, sweating it out on the coffee table. *For the love of Shakespeare.* "Hey, you've eaten all the chocolate fish!"

While she'd been readying for war, he'd gouged out the little piscine shapes, leaving behind wells of vanilla-caramel-marshmallow frozen goodness. Just when her feelings toward him had hooked a left turn into Pity Land.

"Figured you owed me big time," he said with a heartbreakingly sexy grin she felt right down to her curled-up toes.

She scooped out a spoonful and popped it into her mouth. Still good despite the chocolate fish deficiency.

"Gimme your feet, Tess."

Confusion tore at her brain, and she stretched out her legs in some weird Pavlovian response to his soft-spoken order. In a preview of coming attractions, he applied pressure to the arch of her foot with his thumbs, drawing an embarrassingly throaty moan from deep in her throat. Deeper than that.

This was her fantasy right here. A gorgeous man rubbing

her feet while she scarfed down her favorite frozen treat.

"Damn, you're good at that."

"I'm good at lots of things, but I'm afraid the conditions are not to my liking."

"Oh?"

"I do my best work skin-to-skin. Let me take off your socks."

Apparently, they were done talking about Jenna. That was okay. She didn't want to hurt him anymore.

"Okay," she whispered, her inability to deny him as shocking as the electricity sizzling through her while he peeled off one sock. Slowly. Sensuously.

Mistake Number Two.

There was something about the vibe from the minute he had saved her from falling on her ass, an odd static between them. Just like before. She had denied it when it first erupted a year ago. An inappropriate attraction to your friend's fiancé was grounds for disbarment from the Woman Club. Neither did it make a lick of sense. He was uncouth, uneducated, uncivilized. All of their conversations back then had been unholy bicker fests where they charged from the opposite ends of the spectrum, determined not to meet in the middle but to rip pieces out of each other on the drive by.

Now he was here, cradling her naked foot with sandpaper-rough hands. The pleasure as he rubbed his thumbs along the arch of her foot crackled up her calf, through her trembling thigh, and right to the fork of her body. A surge of heat caught a fire in her blood and spread through her veins.

She bit back a moan. *Let him work for it.*

As if knowing she was holding back, those magic fingers upped the stakes. Worked her good. Liquid trouble pooled between her thighs, causing her to shift against the sofa cushion, craving relief.

With a concerted effort, she defogged her brain. The reptilian part of her gray matter clearly had a psychotic break with the rest of her.

"Hunter, why did you come to see me at the theater if you don't want to talk about the past?"

His intent gaze felt like a caress over her sex, confirmation that Hunter Dade turned her on in ways she could barely fathom. Lizard Tess held her breath, waiting. She had high hopes for his next act.

"Are you seeing anybody right now?" he asked, low and husky, as if the night had spoken.

"You mean dating?"

"Dating, leading some guy around by the dick." He paused. "Fucking."

Heat flared in her core. Was he trying to shock her with his crudeness, a wicked contrast to his deferential treatment of her feet? This dickhead had probably taken one look at this house and assumed "rich and sheltered." But twenty-five years on this earth, her movie-set upbringing, and her subsequent life on the boards had prepared her for whatever coarse words Hunter Dade's lips could shape.

"I fail to see how that's any of your business."

His look was one of *we'll see*. What an ass. "I have a proposition for you."

"What kind of proposition?"

"A job."

Surprised, she tugged her foot free. She wasn't qualified for much of anything apart from putting herself out on a limb at the constant risk of falling flat on her face.

"An acting job," he tacked on cryptically into the loaded silence.

"Patron of the arts now?"

"You could say that. How much money do you need to get your theater off the ground?"

Blood stopped moving beneath her skin. "About fifty thousand for the first year. By then we'd hope to be self-sustaining."

The curious flicker he glanced over her affluent surroundings was impossible to miss. "I'll give you a hundred."

"A hundred dollars?"

"A hundred *K*."

She swore the room tilted. Growing up in L.A., the daughter of Hollywood royalty, Tess was not unfamiliar with rich assholes like Hunter Dade throwing large wads of cash at every problem. But since she refused to take a dime of guilt money from her mom, it had become foreign. Unavoidably, her thoughts flew to her living circumstances. Not here, the townhouse of her movie producer ex-stepfather, Brian, which she was currently housesitting while he was at the Warsaw Film Festival, but her humble hovel up in west Rogers Park.

Screw humble, more like broke-dick. The neighborhood was sketchy, her plea to fix the broken lock on the building's front door was currently "under consideration" by her pot-bellied troll of a landlord, and she'd fought raccoons for her ratty sofa.

Hell, she was bone-tired of the daily struggle to keep her head above water.

"What would this job involve?"

"I have a property deal to negotiate in a week. It requires

spending a weekend with a man who has a particular idea of doing business—"

"Hold up, Tex." She scrunched up her knees and hugged them to her chest. "Do you want me to sleep with this guy for your deal?"

"No!" The horror in his voice was matched by his sharp expression. "If you'd let me finish—"

"Well, if you explained it better."

That earned her some first rate glowering. Damn, he was hella sexy when he was mad.

"This man is very happily married and has certain expectations about the people he works with. He doesn't trust single men on the loose around his wife."

"We'd have to get married?"

"No. Jesus, no. We'd have to pretend we're getting there. That we're engaged. In love."

Pretend. As in "acting" because she was…an actress. What else did she think? That she'd be married to this hulk who hated her and would get to spend hot nights being hate-sexed in his hateful, beefcake arms?

Totally thought that, loser.

"We'd visit his ranch in Texas for a weekend. Make nice with him and his wife. Make nice with each other. I get the property he's selling, and you get a hundred thousand dollars."

It sounded too simple. "Why don't you offer him more money?"

"He's not swayed by that, and I have to have this property. That part's nonnegotiable." Steel underlined each word. Why was it that exceptionally wealthy people always had to have more? Success addiction, she supposed. Actors fed off it, too.

Tess McKenzie and success were not on speaking terms lately. She was due.

"We play at being a happy couple and that's it?"

"There are a few other terms I'd like to specify."

Should have known. Patiently, she waited, her breathing at a standstill.

"At least once a day, we argue."

Her throat went as dry as the Sahara. "Argue?"

"Right. We'll decide on a topic and get into it, though knowing you, the topics will fall out naturally." His eyes crinkled around the edges, highlighting extremely attractive laugh lines that might have fooled someone less suspicious. "A little rough 'n' tumble back and forth, get the juices flowing. Would make the couple thing more authentic, don't you think?"

Words failed her, but she had no time to process that because there was more.

"To sweeten the deal, I'll offer daily foot rubs."

Holy shit, this man knew how to grab her attention. Those were not standard bargaining tactics. Arguments, foot rubs... Exactly what was she getting herself into? But the thought of having her theater up and running so soon played the perfect devil's advocate.

She needed to make her own contribution to this negotiation. "I would want something more concrete."

"A hundred *K* isn't concrete enough?"

Her mind scrambled for a bargaining chip, anything so it didn't look like she was completely mercenary. Also, matching his crazy seemed like something he would expect. Something that would please him.

Please him? Where the hell had that come from?

"Ice cream. A year's supply."

Mistake Number Three.

More eye crinkling ensued from Hunter, and she realized her error. *Dumbass.* She could have asked for anything, and that's what she went for?

Oh, well, too late now… She held out her hand to shake on it. He considered it with an amused tilt of his lips.

"You have a lot to learn about business, princess. Now that I've got you on the hook, it's time to play hardball."

"Let's not forget you're the one who needs me," she said quickly.

"Perhaps. But there's the issue of how we feel about each other."

Now we're talking. His intimate tone held sexy promise. "How we feel?"

"We happen to hate each other's guts, Tess."

She blinked, shocked by the certainty in his conclusion. It was one thing to suspect his antagonism toward her, but to have it affirmed aloud hurt like a mother. "Hate is such a strong word."

"Okay, dislike intensely. Maybe with the heat of a thousand suns. If there's that vibe between us, how do I know you can pull it off?"

"I'm an actor. I fake it for a living." That sounded off—and a touch squeaky—but she'd already committed, which is what actors did. "I can pretend to like you for three days."

He grimaced. "Not like. Love. TJ Crandall will spot a fake ten miles off. I need to know if you can get inside your role, Tess. If you can handle being my woman for three days, twenty-four/seven."

Her stomach fluttered, and her girl parts waved a cheery hello. *My woman.* How hot was that?

Except he dislikes you intensely. With the heat of a thousand suns.

"Think I can handle it, Tex," she said, infusing her tone with professionalism, though the moisture between her thighs brought on by his caveman attitude was the opposite of professional.

"Show me."

"Show you what?"

"Show me how you'll handle it." He paused. "Kiss me."

Chapter Four

Gentlemen, start your engines.

There was nothing more gratifying than watching Princess Tess at a loss for words. Well, he could think of a few things — getting his hands on her peaches-and-cream skin was up there — but for now, he'd ride out the sheer pleasure of seeing her knocked off kilter.

"Kiss you." Those green eyes grew wide. "Here? Now?"

"I sure as hell don't mean the first time we have dinner with TJ and Buffy. What if you turn up that snooty nose like you just smelled horse shit? What if you get stage fright? I need to know you can do it."

"You want me to audition? I thought I already had the job."

"We haven't shook hands on it yet. Show me what you've got, Tess."

Time to see how low she was willing to go to get this theater of hers off the ground, though why she needed the cash poked at him. Maybe Daddy or whoever was floating her in this place had cut up her plastic. Maybe she was working out a rebellious streak while she waited for some poor jerk to give in to her every whim. Maybe… He needed to quit worrying about it and just enjoy the show.

"C'mon, honey, I ain't got all day."

A flash of temper ignited in her eyes, but she scooted over all the same and put a hand on his bicep. Even with the barrier of his shirt, her touch sizzled. Tentatively, she inclined her head, leaned in. Breathed deep. With a mild press of her lips, she brushed lightly across his unyielding mouth, and sat back.

His pulse spiked and his blood roared, the kiss no less arousing for its chasteness. If that was Tess when she wasn't trying, he couldn't wait for when she made the effort.

"Hell, I'm not your brother. Do it properly."

There was that flash of anger again, and his cock stirred in response. Taking her would be a pleasure. Making her beg as he fucked her tight, curvy body would be the ultimate prize. Patience was key, though. She had to want him bad. Need what only he could give her. He fought to keep his beast leashed, the victory so sweet he could taste it.

She moved in again. This time, she tugged gently on his lower lip and…laid one on him, moving her mouth over his, working his lips until he had to bite back a moan. Drawing back, she swallowed, eyes blinking with apprehension. "Well?"

He cocked a brow, gave a desultory sniff.

A riot of fire flagged her cheeks. "You're not helping," she grated.

"Hey, simmer down." He regarded her speculatively.

"You know how sometimes you see a movie and you just know Actor X and Actress Y were likely going at it like rabbits between takes in the trailer?"

"Yes?" Tentative hope sounded in that itsy-bitsy word.

"I guess that's not us," he said, battling a smile. "We've got no chemistry."

That set her off. She bolted to a stand and started to pace, though the coffee table didn't really give her much space. Nevertheless, she was stunning, all fire and spirit and hip-swaying power. He'd never had as much fun as when he was fighting with Tess. Which was incredibly arousing and strangely disturbing.

Eyes wide in a hurricane of passion, she stopped, fisted her hands at her hips, and gritted out whatever words her mouth was having trouble forming.

"Get. Out."

Huh?

It took a lot to surprise him, and Tess McKenzie had just managed to pull off the nearly impossible. Seemed he'd underestimated her fury threshold.

"Now, Tess, honey—"

She jabbed a finger of *shut-it* in his direction. "You come in here, with your Texas squinting and your ice-cream fuckery and your amazing foot rubs. You won't even have it out about what happened last year, like a—like a *regular* person. Instead, you demand my help and then expect me to audition like this is a 1950s casting couch. Frankly, Hunter Dade, I'm all assholed out tonight. Fuck your job offer and fuck you!"

Cold dread pooled in his chest, a shocking downshift from the heat he'd been enjoying. She was right. Back at that theater, something had happened to her— He didn't know what, but it was enough to make her quit her job. Now here he was, throwing his weight around, using his power and wealth to force her cooperation. All his life, he lived by a code of respecting women, and in the last ten minutes, every principle had taken a running jump while he preyed on Tess at her lowest point. Just one more example of his trailer park genes coming up trumps.

"Forget what I said, Tess. Forget about…" He waved between them, at a loss to describe his incredibly poor behavior. "If you still want the job, it's yours."

Her eyes sparked in awareness: something had occurred to her, and she was pretty damn pleased about it. "You know what, Mr. Dade? How about *you* audition for *me*?"

Say what now? He shifted on the sofa to accommodate his hard-on, and was making a decent job of it when—*holy shit*—she straddled his lap and placed her hands on his shoulders.

"I should make you pony up a hundred *K* for being such a gold medal asshole."

God, she was as light as air, a slip of a thing with all that female power. Did she have any idea how intoxicating she was, the kind of woman men fought wars over? Died for? She settled in on his thighs, the slight weight of her driving him close to insanity. Desire hummed through him, potent and dangerous.

"Now, Tess," he said, keeping it so casual his bones practically ached with the effort, "I just told you the job is yours."

"Oh, but haven't you heard? I'm hiring, too. This girl's in the market for a guy she can lead around by the dick for, oh, maybe, a weekend. Auditions start tonight."

The surprises, hell, they just kept on coming. Staying level with Tess was going to require fast thinking, which was mighty difficult, considering all the blood he needed for said thought processes was now hurtling south.

"What would this job involve?"

"Only one task. Make. Me. Believe."

"That I'm your fiancé?"

Cue her smile, sly and sexy. First time she'd let him in on that action, too. "That you want me more than your next breath."

If she moved forward a couple inches, his boner would make her believe.

"I've worked with a lot of great actors," she continued with a finger poke in the well of his shoulder, "so if I'm going to take this role on, I need to know *you're* not going to screw it up with your amateur dramatics. Let's see if you've got game."

Oh, he had game all right. Every part of his hardening anatomy was screaming, *put me in, Coach.*

"I dunno," he murmured. "I'd hate to force it."

"Let me help you along, cowboy. I'm used to the director telling me what he wants. So what's my motivation?"

She wanted motivation? *That* he could do. His hands fanned her waist, opening onto her hips, and he worked the silence for a full thirty seconds before he spoke.

"Imagine we're in a room full of strangers, and I brush against you. You're not completely sure it's me, but your body knows 'cause it shivers under my touch. Maybe you're talking to somebody, and you look up because you feel my eyes, heavy on your skin. Your nipples harden. Your panties get wet. Just soak right through."

Negotiating deals was his forte. She didn't stand a chance.

With every word out his mouth, her body was changing. A pulse at the base of her throat fluttered like a hummingbird. Her breaths had started to come in short tugs, and fuck yeah, he just knew from her sexy squirm that slick heat was blooming between those insane thighs.

"We know each other so well," he went on, keeping his voice low, the words crafted to seduce. "Every secret need, every filthy desire, every heartfelt wish. I'm the only one who can do you right, Tess. And in that room of strangers, I'm counting down the minutes to when I'm alone with you. Because I need to know."

"Need to know what?" she whispered. Barely.

"How that freckle on your breast tastes." His hand fisted the hem of her tank top, then yanked it down a couple inches to expose the freckle that needed his tongue on it. Now.

"I'll also be wondering where your other freckles are because that beautiful, creamy skin of yours probably has more. Maybe in hard to reach places. And while I'm thinking about the freckle hunt, I'll be imagining my reward for finding them."

Those big green eyes, flecked with gold sparks, blinked owl-like. "Y-your reward?"

"I'll be thinking about sinking my cock into your soft, wet heat. Stretching you wide while I drive in deep and true. Your greedy pussy gripping me so tight I might not be able to hold on long enough to get you off first."

She moaned, the sound so needful that his cock punched painfully against his zipper.

He leaned in, his lips grazing her ear. "You understand

your motivation now, honey?"

He had scarcely enough time to lever his head back before their mouths joined in a crush of heat and desire. Hunger for her took over, a deep-seated craving that rattled and rolled every muscle, vein, and cell. In that moment, the who, what, and why of his payback scheme was smothered under the blanket of something more dangerous and all-consuming.

Just her.

Just Tess.

Hunter's mouth plundered and conquered, his tongue thrusting in a luxurious sweep that had Tess clutching at his shoulders and holding on for dear life. They kissed like they fought: wild, uninhibited, with bite. Maybe not healthy but she couldn't recall ever feeling this good, and after the night she'd had, it was just what the sex doctor ordered.

No chemistry?

No freaking way.

Tess pulled back for air, a much needed oxygen influx to get her bearings. The point had been made. They could seal the deal and move forward safe in the knowledge their romantic compatibility would not be in question.

High five, universe.

But that kiss did more than turn her into a puddle of lust. It terrified her. Not because of how soul-searingly good it was, but because kisses like that don't just happen. Kisses like that implied history and connection and bone-deep knowledge, and it made her question everything that had existed between them before. Had something lain dormant all this time, waiting for the planets to align and bring him here to this sofa?

Mistake number…. She'd lost count. Breathless, she stared at him. "Well, that was…something."

Those dark blues stared back, seeking access to the secrets his tongue had yet to discover. Getting lost in those pools would be so easy. So hazardous. She wanted pleasure: mindless, trouble-busting pleasure, not this heavy emotion like a dumbbell in her chest. She needed to escape, but his provocative words froze her in place, a relentless assault of dirty talk that played back in her decelerating brain.

I'll be thinking about sinking my cock into your soft, wet heat.

She raised her body up a few inches, intending to separate from him, no, *needing* to, before she let this go further. The motion dragged his hands across her abdomen. That gentle touch sent a frisson of need down her spine that sparked to flame in her sex.

Stretching you wide while I drive in deep and true.

With eyes so heated she wondered how she was still solid, he watched her intently. This had to…had to stop.

Your greedy pussy gripping me so tight I might not be able to hold on long enough to get you off first.

She pressed back against his hands, a blatant invitation to…what? Both of Hunter's magical thumbs dipped to form a *V* over her mound.

Oh, that's what.

She was in way over her head here. She'd always suspected he was far too much for Jenna to handle, and this confirmed it. What did it say about her that she was so on board?

Trouble brewed in his stormy eyes, and he shook his head and gently pushed her away a few inches. "Tess, this has epically terrible idea written all over it. I shouldn't have spoken to you like that. You've had a bad night, what with losing your job and all."

And all, the details of which he had no idea. This further evidence of his protectiveness completely undid her. Making this choice, with the one man who could protect her body and destroy every last defense, made her dizzy with lust—and power. Didn't she deserve this pleasure? The last year had been the worst of her life, looking after Gran before the bravest woman Tess knew had finally succumbed to the big *C.* The last month had been spent fending off visual assaults from audience members and the hands-eyes shudder combo of creepy Derek. She lived in a shithole in a crappy neighborhood.

Any second now, the moment would pass. No more kisses. No more panty-melting dirty talk. No more Hunter. She sent a plea up to the sex gods. Could she keep him for a little longer?

"Then turn it into a good night, Hunter." And to make sure he understood she was choosing this, she leaned back and peeled off her tank top.

Male appreciation hardened his features from doubt to certainty. Boobs, the best negotiation strategy of them all. She thanked the Lord and her genetics for her great rack.

"Touch me," she ordered.

A slight lip curl was his response, and for the briefest moment, she feared he might reject her. But then his thumb traced over her freckle, almost like he had to check if it was real. If she was real. He filled his coarse palm with the weight of her breast, the contrast between their skin textures enough to renew the wet warmth in her panties.

"Tess," he said thickly.

"Please, Hunter." Touch her there. Make it better. *Just please.* Unable to stand the suspense, she dug her fingers into his tightly-loomed shoulder muscles and covered his mouth with hers.

Oh, sweet Jesus.

Thoughts vaporized. Her spine dissolved. Her muscles went AWOL. Stellar timing because it gave her the perfect excuse to mold her boneless body to his. Every part of her strained to touch every part of him: her aching breasts, her clenching thighs, her sensitive sex.

Hunter's large hands dug into her ass, eliminating what little space remained between them. Those deadly weapons moved over her expertly, teasing her to mindlessness, metal to her magnet. First, her ass, and then back to her waist. He was everywhere, but it was still not enough. His thumbs pushed down in the crease where her thighs met her hips. Down…down…

Usually it took her a while to reach that peak, but she knew on the first touch of his hand over her aching, fabric-covered core that she'd be gone in a few mind-melting seconds. The moment he had shown up at the theater, the foreplay had begun. Every word and gesture since, even his chocolate fish larceny, had hiked her desire higher.

One thick thumb now worked the fabric's seam between her legs, the same talented thumb that drove her to distraction during that foot rub. His other hand held her hip steady, anchored in the here and now.

"Not. Enough," she moaned, desperation for skin-on-skin shredding her nerves. "Please. Your fingers. Inside me."

On a barked curse, he yanked her yoga pants halfway down her thighs, her panties with them, and plunged one—oh, God, *yes,* two—fingers inside her.

She needed this. She needed *him.*

He stilled his fingers, letting her body adjust to the pleasurable invasion. "Your gorgeous tits, Tess. Want them. In my mouth."

She heard a negotiation in there. Those thick, orgasm-producing fingers wouldn't be doing their job until she plated up something in return. Luckily, it was an offer she had no intention of refusing.

She slipped her breast free of one of the lacy cups, then plumped and teased his mouth with its rosy tip. Watching the desire flare in his eyes put her right on the edge; the first touch of his hot tongue to her nipple almost sent her over. "Oh, God, oh, God."

"Ride my fingers, Tess," he rasped against her slicked-up breast as his fingers dragged back and forth through her swollen folds. "Imagine it's my tongue. My cock."

The build of pleasure was so intense she almost pulled back. He sensed it, knew it before she did. Deepening the hot, wet suckle of her breast, he applied more friction where she needed it over the nerve-packed flesh of her clit.

No mercy.

"There, yes, God, *yes!*"

She imploded, the force of the orgasm dragging throaty moans from her mouth, and to her mortification, his name. Several times. She fell against his hand, riding long shivering pulses of pleasure, the aftershocks rocking her in sensitive twitches. Coming back to herself seemed to take forever.

They stayed that way for a few heavenly, breath-gasping moments. After what had happened back at the theater, it was so good to wrest back control—by losing it in the most delicious way possible. Her personal version of *Take Back The Night*.

"Well… That was something," he said with a smile she felt curving against her neck.

Hell, yeah.

"You've got the job, Tex."

He laughed softly into her neck, and that sound so perfectly encapsulated this moment between them, a temporary cessation of hostilities. But it couldn't last. She wanted to see him wrecked like he'd done to her. Drunk on her newfound power, she crept her hands down his contoured chest. Making her move, staking her claim. His eyelids fell to half-mast over pleasure-clouded eyes. They both knew where this was going.

Apparently so did the universe.

The electronica strains of "The Yellow Rose of Texas" cut into the sex-charged silence. *Really?*

"I need to get that," he said darkly, no hesitation.

Most guys on the verge of getting lucky would ignore a late night call unless they were doctors or drug dealers. Was there such a thing as a property emergency? With one hand, he extracted his phone from his jacket, draped over the arm of the sofa. His other hand still curved around her hip possessively, locking her in place over his impressive arousal, and preventing her from unhinging her highly sensitive body.

"Dade," he said into the phone.

Her yoga pants were still down, her breasts front and

center. The twenty tense seconds while he listened was more than enough time for Tess to rack up frequent flyer miles of regrets, but then she remembered how he tasted and talked, and best of all, felt, against her sex.

Hard. For her.

His eyelids shuttered in what looked like relief. "I'll be there in a couple hours." On ending the call, thoughts chased each other across his face.

A couple hours? That didn't sound like an emergency. It sounded like more than enough time to…

"Gotta go, honey."

"Oh." Surprise dulled her reflexes, but he was patient, waiting while she clambered off him.

He unfolded his long, lean body to a stand and slipped on his jacket while she fumbled with her pants and tank top. When she had covered up, he held out his hand. "Walk me to the door."

Without hesitation, she let his large, male grip swallow her hand and guide her to the door. One sock on, one sock off. "Is everything okay?"

He gave a short nod, evidently distracted by whatever he had heard on the other end of the line. "Just some business I have to take care of."

It would be foolish and unaccountably needy to take offense at his sudden coolness. Instead, she aimed for casual. Hot guy, world-class orgasm, no biggie.

"Thanks for seeing me home and for…" Giving her the best *O* of her life. For being here when she needed…with what she needed.

"No problem. Clear your schedule for next weekend. I'll call you with the details." His tone was all business. At the door, he worked the deadbolt a couple times. "And lock this the second I leave."

The space around her heart constricted at this demonstration of his protective streak. Lord, it was going to be the death of her. Stepping in, he gentled her jaw and swiped her lip with his thumb. Her knees melted.

"This isn't why I drove you home, you know," he murmured.

Humiliation flared. Tess did not do relationships, having seen the havoc they wreaked on her mom's life—six stepdads and numerous "uncles" will do that. Unfortunately, men were necessary for a twenty-first century hetero gal's fulfillment. Her preference was to be upfront about her sexual needs. A little fast, a lot dirty, and no need to text her the day after. There should be no shame attached, but tonight, she had pushed Hunter into giving her a hand—literally—and now he was calling her out on it.

"I know. I'm sorry I provoked you."

His eyes widened. "No, don't ever be sorry for that. You've provided fantasy material for every shower jerk off for the foreseeable future. I meant that you're not what I expected. In a good way." He looked annoyed. With her? With himself?

Her mind blurred with an image of Hunter in the shower, slick and soapy, moaning her name as he stroked himself. And now she had a healthy balance of hot Texan in her personal spank bank, *thankyouverymuch*.

"You're not what I expected, either," she choked out.

He brushed his lips across hers, a sinful stroke of fire that licked her core and had her craving more. No doubt, his evil plan.

"One more thing."

"What?" she whispered. Oh, God, he needed to leave now or fuck her raw against the Mark Rothko in the foyer.

"Hold off on touching yourself until I see you again. Think you could manage that for me?"

Her breath caught. She wanted to remember this moment later after whatever was happening between them had flat-lined and died.

"Tess, you get what I'm sayin'?"

"Yes, I get it. And yes… I can do that." Swallowing her heart, she wondered if she had made a deal with the devil. "You, too."

He made a rough sound, all growly and hot. It shot sparks all the way to her toes and radiated back up to hit every highly sensitive nerve ending.

"Me, too." And on that, he was gone, leaving the beautifully appointed townhouse feeling grim and poky and unbelievably cold.

Chapter Five

Hunter dumped his overnight bag inside the door of his office in the South Wacker Tower and trudged to the sofa, ready to collapse. The floor to ceiling windows let in far too much of the afternoon October light, but no matter. Not even the breathtaking view overlooking the Chicago River as it snaked its way to Lake Michigan could keep him from shutting his heavy-lidded eyes.

"You're back."

But Brody Kane could.

Hunter sighed as he slumped against the plush sofa cushions. "Stunning deduction, Captain Fucking Obvious." With one eye peeking open, because dammit, he was going to get some shuteye if it killed him, he peered at Brody, better known as the brains of Score Property. Or maybe it was the fact he wore glasses. The Clark Kent vibe made him the ultimate chick magnet, but he wore his nerd credentials like a badge of honor and never took advantage of the women lining up to polish his light saber. Hunter didn't know the full story, but apparently celibacy was his superpower since his version of Lois Lane screwed him over.

"How's your mom?" Brody asked.

The mere mention of Cecile was like ice water to Hunter's senses. Straightening, he ran a hand through his shorn hair. It felt grimy, like he'd brought half the dusty acreage of the Southwest home.

How was his mom? Bruised, belligerent, pissed to all hell at him, but otherwise same old Mom. She'd dropped in for her monthly visit to the drunk tank after taking a face plant in the parking lot of the local dive bar. Likely, she took a swing at someone who had looked at her crooked. His abiding childhood memories were of a wasted Cecile picking fights with the other residents at Lindo Pines, a place that was neither pretty nor piney. Trailer parks needed optimism, and it started with the name.

"She's home," he said in a voice that made it clear this conversation had no legs. He'd picked her up, cleaned her cuts, and had the same talk he had with her every damn time. *Let me help you.* Repeating that other well-worn appeal, where he asked her to forgive him for what happened to Alison, only spiked her Irish, so he'd abandoned it years ago.

Thankfully, further discussion on the topic was cut short when their office manager, Emma Strickland—in truth their office queen because she was regal, efficient, and unflappable—curved her head around the door.

"Two or three, Mr. Dade?" she asked, perfectly anticipating his needs.

"Three," he muttered.

An elegant brunette whose sensible suits covered up

more skin than they revealed, Emma padded in and handed him three extra-strength Tylenol capsules and a glass of water. Hunter bet she had a decent body under that shapeless skirt and chin-high blouse, but she wasn't letting anyone in on her secrets. He and Flynn had tried to get her to loosen up and call them by their first names, but she insisted on the mister.

He downed the pain relievers in one swallow. Traveling always gave him a headache.

Emma offered a supportive smile. "I had already requested the rest of this afternoon off, so unless there's something else…"

Hunter opened his mouth to answer, then clamped it shut one second later when he realized she didn't give a flying fuck about his opinion. By the looks of the wide-eyed stare she leveled at Brody, the only stamp of approval necessary was from him.

"Mr. Kane, do you need anything before I leave?" *Me on the desk? The floor? Against the window?*

Distractedly, Brody looked up from one of the contracts in his hand. "No, Miss Strickland, that'll be all."

Brody was the only one who called her Miss Strickland. All that Miss and Mister between them— There was something weirdly kinky about it. She gave a puppy-eyed blink and headed out as quietly as she came.

"What'd I miss?" Hunter asked.

Brody jerked back from some faraway place with a rub of his hand over his mouth. Ah, not so unaffected by Miss Strickland after all. "I beat Flynn's ass in HORSE, and he's still sobbing about it. Contracts came in from the lawyer. Blue Point, the North Shore development, Crandall." He laid the legal documents on Hunter's desk.

Hunter had a meeting at four, which left two hours for a nap and time to shave and shower the grit off him. Swinging his legs, boots and all, up on the sofa, he stretched out.

"Shut the door on the way out, bro."

Brody cleared his throat significantly. One of Hunter's eyelids crept open, hauled up by an imaginary fishhook.

"Seems there's another contract here. One Hunter Dade"—Brody pointed at Hunter—"that'd be you. And one Tess McKenzie." His business partner picked up a blue-covered loose-leaf, about an eighth of the thickness of the usual property contracts. "In consideration of services rendered, Hunter Dade will compensate Tess McKenzie one hundred thousand dollars to be paid on return to Chicago from Kerrville, Texas no later than October thirty-first. During the weekend of October twenty-third to twenty-fifth, Hunter Dade will give Tess McKenzie at least one foot rub per day."

Brody delivered a glance so disapproving Hunter almost cared. "You haven't specified an upper limit there, so you could be in trouble. Thumb cramps." He turned back to the contract. "The parties will engage in at least one argument per day—again no upper limit—on topics to be mutually decided."

Hunter closed his eyes. Absolutely divine. "Keep reading. If I wasn't sleepy before, that should do the trick."

"Hunter, what the… I mean…"

With his eyelids resting, Hunter was blind to Brody's precise actions, but he guessed it probably involved scrubbing a hand through his dark brown, floppy hair and taking off his glasses for a vigorous wipe-down. He let the man get there by himself.

"The…the fuck?" Brody finally managed.

"Pretty smooth, Dade," Hunter heard from the doorway. Ah, hell, he wasn't getting any zees now. His eyes creaked open to take in Flynn propping up the doorframe with arms crossed and mouth mocking. "So you bagged the maid of honor." He sounded like a proud father.

"The maid of honor?" Brody asked, brows slammed together. "Explain."

Flynn filled him in on how Hunter had ran into Tess at her show and then looked to Hunter for details on how to finish the story. "You put it to her? The proposal, that is. Unless you really did put it to her."

There'd be no come-and-tell from Hunter, though the memory of Tess flying apart against his hand was as potent as if she were straddling him right this minute. Her whimpers, her moans, her cries of release, still echoed in his ear. Jesus, he couldn't wait to hear those same sounds while he was moving deep inside her.

"She said yes to my proposal, if that's what you're asking."

Flynn cocked his head, looking more thoughtful than usual. Unlike the analytical Brody, Flynn was all instinct, which Hunter imagined came in real handy in his Special Forces days. "And you sorted out your differences?"

Not exactly, though she certainly thought so. "We've risen above it."

"And now you're going to spend three days with her," Flynn said. "I'd high five you, dude, but I'm too lazy to walk over to that sofa."

Brody frowned. "So let me get this straight. You've hired an actress to play your fiancée for the weekend, and in consideration of those services, she's going to get a hundred thousand dollars."

"And foot rubs and ice cream. I'll get the arguments, but I think she likes them, too." Hell yeah, she did. Those pinches of color on her cheeks when he got her mad were a preview of how much fun they were about to have.

"And you're planning to have sex with her?"

Hunter jerked short, not liking his boy's tone. Neither did he like that Brody was still frowning, because when he frowned past five seconds it was bad news. It meant he'd seen a kink in a plan that no one else had caught.

"Most definitely," Hunter said decisively because that was half the battle there.

Brody shook his head. *No, no, you fucker. Unshake it, now.* "You can't. Well, you can, but it doesn't say good things about you if you do."

"What the hell are you jawin' on about?" Flynn snapped at Brody. Might be some residual tension there from getting whupped at hoops. "If they want to do the nasty, what reason could they have for not going for it?"

Brody shot Flynn a look of infinite patience. He really could be such a smart-ass. "Just a hundred thousand of 'em."

His tiredness history, Hunter shot up off the sofa as realization thumped him like a log. He was paying her. A lot of money.

"She's my employee."

"Give the boy a sucker. Independent contractor, actually," Brody said, much too smug, "but yes, that's the upshot of it. While there's nothing to stop you both legally, the ethical implications are a minefield."

Shit, shit, shit. How the fuck was he supposed to make her beg if he couldn't get her all hot and bothered? Fantasies of playing footsie under the table at Crandall's, then following up with hands all over her body froze in his brain. End of the line. No can do. Because even if she *thought* she wanted him, how could she separate that from the great wad of cash he was going to give her? She might feel obliged to fuck him because he had all the money. All the power.

Like the other night. *Quadroshit.* So yeah, she'd flipped that table, recast the power dynamic, and he had no doubt she was in control—as much as a woman in the midst of overwhelming sexual ecstasy could be. But now, he wanted her pleading for the sweet release that came when his working-class cock was pounding the ever-loving superiority out of her.

Well, so much for that plan. It was supposed to end up with upper-crust Tess desperate, begging— And somehow this scheme had gifted her the I'm-headin'-to-the-light orgasm and left him with blue balls the size of freaking cantaloupes.

He picked up his phone and stared at it awhile when really he wanted to hurl it through that floor-to-ceiling window.

"Maybe it's for the best," Flynn said. "I know you think buying that land is going to make things better but"—he shot a tentative glance at Brody—"what if it doesn't? You get it and then what? It won't bring Alison back."

Flynn flinched at the cutting look Hunter knifed his way.

"If you're not behind me, say so." He flicked a similarly barbed glance to Brody. "Say it now."

Brody pushed his glasses up his nose and shrugged. "Of course we're behind you. When all's said and done, it makes business sense. It's prime real estate, and the mixed use potential is through the roof."

Neither of them needed to elaborate any further. It might make business sense, but emotionally it was a tangled web that threatened to put the final nail in the relationship coffin with his mother.

Grimacing, he scrolled through his contacts.

"What about the actress?" Flynn asked. "You calling that off?"

Calling it off was not an option. He needed that land, and Tess was his best shot. As for that payback… Maybe denying her for a while would be its own reward. It would probably kill him, too, but hell if misery didn't enjoy a little company.

"What do you mean 'not engage in sexual relations'?"

Tess blinked a few times at the black-and-white print, waiting for the words to magically transform before her disbelieving eyes, but the song remained the same. One hundred thousand dollars. Check. Foot rubs, arguments, ice cream. All as it should be. And then this gem:

The parties to this contract will not engage in sexual relations for the duration of the agreement.

"I think it's very clear," Hunter said in a strained voice that was still perfectly audible above the low hum of the Learjet's engines. Just the two of them in the cozy, leathery confines, winging their way to Texas for a fun and—she had hoped—filthy weekend.

Yesterday, she had met Jenna for brunch at M. Henry. Once they'd covered the obligatory catch up on Steve's stamp collection and Jenna's latest charitable cause, Tess casually dropped in a, "so, any objections to me getting na-key with your former fiancé this weekend?" The code of chicks-before-dicks required it, but even now an uncomfortable heat pooled in her chest as she recalled her friend's reaction.

Jenna—so sweet, so cheat-y, so wrong for dirty-talking Hunter Dade—had blushed to the roots of her perfectly layered blond hair and blinked in genuine shock. *Why, Tess, you said he was a roughneck whose second car was probably a monster truck.* Yes, she had said that and a whole lot more. What a superior bitch she had been.

The brunch interrogation lasted from coffee to check at which point Jenna paid with her daddy-issued credit card. *My treat, Tess,* then regally gave her blessing to the entire smutty enterprise. *I want Hunter to be happy.* And Tess had planned to make him very happy indeed. She had shaved above the knee, packed her suitcase with her skimpiest lingerie, and the instructions on the Sexy Weekend Fun Box said, "Just Add Texan." What she had not expected was Hunter putting her on a Tex-free diet.

"You might think it's clear, but I need it explained to me."

He strummed his long fingers on the armrest. "Given that there's a lot of money in play, we— I thought this would be for the best. That way, there's no confusion."

She jumped on his stumble. "Who's we?"

His expression was pained. "My business partners."

"You discussed *not* having sex with me with your business partners?"

"Now, Tess—"

"You discussed how you would not be getting down

and dirty with me, and you felt it necessary to put it in a contract. What if we have sex anyway?" What if it had gone the way she had expected all along? Every heated look, touch, promise fulfilled beyond her wildest dreams. "Does that void the contract? Do I not get my money?"

Bewilderment improved his hotness by a factor of ten thousand. Damn his sexy confusion. "Of course not. As long as you stay the entire weekend and play your part, you get paid. The clause is there so you don't feel pressured. So you don't feel I'm paying—"

"Me to have sex with you?"

He gave a slow, southern gentleman nod.

"Are you worried I'll turn into mush and fall for you? Because newsflash, your penis is nowhere near that powerful, Hunter. I'm not interested in a relationship."

His handsome features turned to granite. "I'm not good enough for Jenna, so I couldn't possibly be relationship material for you. Is that it?"

"No—no, that's not what I mean." Heat scalded her cheeks and that uncomfortable sensation in her chest came back. The one that reminded her of his hurt at losing sweet, perfect Jenna. Never mind that her friend was *cheating* on Hunter. "You and Jenna would have...destroyed each other."

He stared, undiluted disdain hardening his eyes. "Is that what you told her, princess?"

She swallowed back a near-hysterical laugh because Tess's life was so unprincess-like it wasn't even funny. Damn, she wanted to strangle Jenna for messing with Hunter's mind, but the woman was still her friend. No matter how wrong she had been to string Hunter along, it wasn't Tess's place to tarnish his perception of his former fiancée — or melt that chip on his shoulder he had about people with college degrees or an appreciation for the Arts.

"I told her it couldn't work between you."

His brows slammed together. "Guess I have my uses, though. Or maybe that's how you view all men."

"Is that so surprising?"

"I'm just a country boy, so it's mighty hard for me to wrap my head around you city girls." His headshake was more sad than confused. "A woman who doesn't want a ring on her finger after that screaming orgasm I gave her a week ago? Hell, I must be losing my touch."

She rolled her eyes indulgently, relieved they appeared to be back to the flirtatious vibe between them.

"I didn't scream, you ass."

"Nah, you made those soulful little sounds in your throat. More like, *Unh, unh, oh, oh…oh, Huuuunter*." He had *not* just mimicked her *O* sounds. His eyes gleamed, smug with it. "So why don't you want a relationship?"

That sudden change up from annoyingly sexy to super serious caught her off guard. She lifted her shoulder in a half shrug. "Having some fun with no strings or expectations is more my style. Most guys find being with an actress tough. All that drama."

"Ah, I see." He shot her a look that said he did see — right through her flimsy defense. "Someone did a number on you."

"You assume because I want strings-free, it must be because some guy hurt me? God, the arrogance." So her man record was wickedly poor. Her last fling ended when the guy got too clingy, and the one before that. Actors, both of them, the neediest species on the planet. It was hard to get on board with a man who thought your best asset was you couldn't compete for the same roles.

"Just an educated guess. Most people are looking for someone who'll treat them right and won't screw them over."

Maybe. But think of all the hay you had to pluck out of your underwear to find that needle. A long time ago, Tess had decided to keep her body open but a No Trespassing sign pinned over her heart, and it worked. She wasn't about to turn over and expose her soft underbelly, especially for the likes of Hunter Dade.

He considered her so closely her skin itched, probably some well-honed negotiating strategy where silence was supposed to make her spill her guts. Obligingly, she caved like a cheap suitcase.

"I've seen what happens when you rely on men for your self-worth. My mother did that. Still does it. She claims she doesn't need a man, but then the next minute she's got a new jerk in tow, and she's letting him walk all over her."

"Ding dong," he drawled, referring to her special ring-tone for Deb. Trust him to remember that. "I don't know whether to apologize for the mistakes of my gender or delve deeper into your mommy issues. Which should we cover first?"

"I'd much rather talk about the *uses* of your gender," she said, moving them back to the problem at hand. No way did she want Hunter Dade mining her psyche. The guy did not need any more ammunition.

"Well, my mama always said I should aim to be useful, but that doesn't change what's happening here. I respect you, and I don't want you to feel you owe me that gorgeous body of yours in exchange for a payday."

Gorgeous body. That she could definitely work with, though a niggling thought gnawed at her consciousness. "What about a few days ago? We'd already discussed money before the "audition." You didn't have any qualms about—"

"Making you come hard and fast?" Arousal flared his nostrils and flagged his cheeks with color. The memory of his hands on her, drawing her to a blistering peak, flooded the space between them and the sensitive area between her thighs.

"I apologize for taking advantage," he murmured. "You were vulnerable, and then I threw a bunch of Benjamins into the mix—"

No freaking way. She shot to a stand, dumping the contract to the floor. "Don't you dare apologize for that. I knew exactly what I was doing and so did you. We're consenting adults, Hunter, and I call bullshit."

Slowly, she moved toward him, but because it was only two feet of space, it wasn't quite the siren walk she had intended. Wobbling on the heels she needed lessons in wearing didn't help, but she had worn these and the lace-bordered thigh highs because she knew he liked that look on her. Today, she was Tess the sexpot. Tonight, she would inhabit the role of Tess the loving fiancée. Tomorrow, who knew?

Laying a hand on his broad shoulder for leverage, she straddled him. The flex of his holy-crap muscles beneath her palm, all that power and strength, floored her. A man who could both pleasure and protect.

Not that she needed protecting. She blinked that intruding thought away.

"Tess…" he growled, trailing off as his hand fanned her

waist. Didn't try to stop her, though. His tight grip both held her at bay and prevented the retreat she had no intention of making.

"You think I can't separate this out? That I'm so addled by your riches, I'll lift my skirt"—she raised said skirt above the edges of the stockings—"and poor lil ole me will give it up because I'm worried I won't get paid if I don't?"

The hand not clenching her hip coasted along her thigh deliberately, taking his sweet time. The heat of his touch blistered all the way to her clit. Boy, this man did it for her like no other. He hooked a finger under the top of one stocking. Rolled it down an inch. Hissed on an inhale.

Hunter likey.

"I think money changes everything," he ground out. "You're effectively my employee, and for me to expect you'll sleep with me would be wrong."

"I know you don't expect it." But *she* did, and it was about the only thing that had powered her through this last week. "If I thought you expected it, I wouldn't be here."

The man had done nothing but protect and respect her since he'd shown up in that theater, unknowingly scaring off Derek. Clearly he didn't understand how much it meant to have control over her pleasure that night and who would give it. Instead, he was apologizing for taking advantage. She scooted in closer until her knees touched the back of the seat. Until her lace-shielded sex lay flush against his erection, which jerked in response. *Holy wow.* He made a very male sound in his throat.

"What pisses me off, Hunter, is you think I'm incapable of making this decision for myself."

"Don't twist my words, Tess. If I say this is about respect, it is. It's not a shot at your female power."

In a devastating feat of Hunter manliness, he stood, lifting her with him, and deposited her in the opposite seat. "Hope that's clear."

"Of course. You've cleared it right up," she said, still seething at his unmitigated gall. Did he think she was some hapless ingénue who shouldn't get a vote on her own sexual choices? Oh, a woman never got tired of having a man explain something so it made sense to her peanut-sized female brain.

She scooped up the contract from the floor, making sure she dipped low enough to display her cleavage. *Oops.* At the subtle shift in his seat, she cheered a mental home run.

"Doesn't matter anyway," she said.

"Hmm?" He picked up a magazine from a side table and flipped the pages casually, right side up. *Kudos, Hunter Dade.*

"Have it your way."

He looked up. Held her gaze. Did his smoldering thing. "Is that some reverse psychology bullshit they teach you in college, or did you read it in *Cosmo*?"

"I can take care of my own needs, cowboy. We city girls know how to adapt to any situation." Quickly, she scanned the contract again and held the pen over the blank line where her John Hancock should go. Hunter's confident scrawl was already in place on the left side, egging her on. Even his signature taunted her with its masculinity.

"I still get paid even if we have hot, sweaty, the-best-lay-you've-ever-had sex?"

Not a muscle in the rock-hewn planes of his face moved. He just kept his gaze trained on *SkyMall for Billionaires* or *Texan Tycoons* or whatever the hell he was pretending to read. Guy was good.

"Even if I make you come so hard your ears are ringing for days." He flipped a page, still refusing to meet her daggered gaze. "But we won't be having sex, Tess."

Right, because he respected her, and this contract clause was for her protection. Poor Hunter. She almost felt sorry for him.

Chapter Six

CAUTION. ROUGH ROAD AHEAD.

With Hunter's looming silence as they moved closer to their destination, the road sign kicking off the driving portion of their journey rang more and more resonant. Every now and then he'd point out an interesting rock formation or the odd looking vegetation that punctuated the terrain. Yucca, cedars, Texas live oak. Tess tried to draw him out with questions about where he had grown up, only to get a tight-lipped response of "Over that way," with a wave to the west. It was like trying to squeeze water out of the prickly pear cacti that dotted the landscape. Even her A-material about Texas having viniculture—they passed a couple of vineyards on the way—got nothing.

Texas. Wine. *Nothing.*

About thirty minutes after they had touched down at the airport in Kerrville, they pulled into a driveway leading to a humongous ranch with a long, low profile, large windows, and a slate roof. In L.A., this kind of brute footprint on the landscape smacked of ostentation; here it was more of a reclaiming.

"Wow, they sure do everything bigger in Texas," she said, falling back on the cliché to provoke a reaction.

Still nothing from that hunk to her left. *Bigger in Texas.* She had laid that one up perfectly.

"Stop this car," she said. "Now."

The car ground to a halt on the gravel, and concern skewed his rugged features to the cragginess of one of his favorite rock formations. "What's wrong?"

"You tell me."

He had rolled up his shirt sleeves, revealing dark hair that contrasted tantalizingly with his tanned, muscled arms. She took advantage of his distress and rubbed his bare forearm.

"What gives, Tex? Has it finally hit that thick skull of yours that you've got three days of sexy torture ahead of you courtesy of Yours Truly?"

His gorgeous smile lifted her heart. "Resisting your charms is going to be mighty hard, but that's not it." He stared off into the distance. "See that fence?"

Following his gaze, her eyes landed on a long, white fence encircling what looked like a paddock. There were no horses, but she could imagine them trotting around on another day, frolicking or whatever horses did for kicks.

"I built that. I used to work here as a kid. Odd jobs, putting up barns, mucking out stables." He huffed out a heavy breath. "It's just strange to be back."

Every minute in his presence impressed her more and made her cringe at her past snobbery. "You've come a long way."

He looked at her sharply, a tight set to his mouth. "Sometimes it feels like I'm spinning my wheels. You know how you think you've let go of things, but something—a sound, a smell, a smile—reminds you that you've not let go of shit?"

An empathy-shaped ache bloomed in her chest at his honesty. She knew exactly where Hunter was coming from. Putting an entire continent between her and her mother did nothing to soothe the sting of betrayal that Tess still felt.

"What haven't you let go of, Hunter, other than shit?"

"I made a mistake when I was younger, and someone else paid the price. I can't undo that, but this weekend I hope to make some of it right." He held her gaze boldly. "Winning is the best therapy."

How buying a piece of land could erase that hollowness in his eyes was not computing with her right now. On the flight, she had learned that he grew up outside Kerrville, worked construction, had some lucky breaks, and founded Score Property with his business partners four years ago. A typical self-made man story, except she knew there were untold chapters in the tense line of his shoulders and the whitened knuckles as he gripped the steering wheel.

"What was the mistake you made, Hunter? And how does buying a piece of land make it right?"

"It's nothin' for you to worry about, Tess." He flicked a gaze to the house and back to her, and she could see him grasping for his good humor. "You ready to act your sweet ass off?"

"I was born ready, Tex."

"You know, calling a Texan guy Tex in Texas is sort of redundant, Yankee girl."

She thought on it a moment. "What would you prefer? Baby cakes? Snookums?"

"Damn, you would." His smile returned. She almost believed it. "Open the glove compartment. I got something for you."

As she lowered the cover, the easily recognizable shape of a jewelry box stole her breath. When had he slipped an engagement ring by her? With fingers as thick as sausages, she fumbled with it, already knowing it would be big and brash like Jenna's.

Oh, God, maybe it *would be* Jenna's.

Needing to get this over with as quickly as possible, she wrenched it open before her butterfingers lost grip again.

She gasped. This wasn't the expected three-carat Princess cut solitaire but a smaller oval sapphire set in a diamond halo, the warm glow of the jewel a perfect match for Hunter's midnight eyes.

"Figured I'd get something that suits you." He plucked the ring out of the velvet bed and held up her hand. Reverently, to her mind, he slipped it on her wedding finger. Somehow, he'd guessed perfectly her ring size.

Her left hand felt like if didn't belong to her. Heavy. Weighted with expectation. Hunter still held it and stared at the ring with an ever-changing carousel of expressions on his face. As if he was auditioning, and the director had told him: *Show me confused. Show me awe.*

Show me longing.

Her emotions blended into one goopy, flavorless mess. He was thinking of Jenna and the life he had been denied with her.

"You like it?"

All she could do was nod. *You did good, Hunter Dade.*

"I know you're dying to make some crack about my bad luck with engagements, Tess, so out with it."

"Not at all," she mumbled, her heart squeezing that he would think her so crass. To him, she was still the insensitive bull in the china shop of his dreams. Swallowing a rock of emotion the size of the monstrous gem she didn't get, she turned to the window and dug her nails into her palms to stave off threatening tears. There was no reason why she should want to cry right now, except she did and that was reason enough.

Take deep breaths. You're about to go on stage. The role of your life.

He drove the car around back and pulled up to a door that would have been epic on the front of a regular house. Before she could get her shit together, Hunter was out and opening the passenger door.

"Come on, honey," he said, holding out his hand.

She'd never tire of those manners, though she wouldn't mind a little less respect later. Taking his outstretched hand, she let him pull her up into his rock-hard side.

"Hunter Bean, get on over here and give me a hug."

Hunter Bean? A small woman, barely coming halfway up Hunter's chest, launched herself at him.

"Marta, you still here? I thought you were gonna retire to a beach house in Galveston." Enveloping the woman in his big grip, he kissed the crown of her dark head and held on to her for an extra long beat.

"I ain't cut out for island livin'," the woman scoffed, slapping his chest, a move that required her to reach up. She stood back, assessing him with a maternal eye or something very close. "You're big enough to bear hunt with a branch, Hunter Bean. You sure come a long way from the skinny kid gettin' your hands all cut up buildin' that barn."

Hunter laughed, robust and deep. "Marta, I want you to meet Tess McKenzie, my fiancée. Tess, Marta runs things around here."

The older woman cuffed him on the arm again, a mix of pride and embarrassment on her weathered face. She could have been anywhere between fifty and seventy-five.

"Hi, Marta," Tess said, shaking her hand. She had a terrifyingly strong grip for one so tiny. "Can't wait to hear all the dirt you've got on this guy."

"Three days won't be enough for all I gotta say." She divided a look between the two of them. "She's mighty pretty. Far too good for a rascal like you."

"Don't I know it?" Hunter's gaze slid to Tess, a strange shift of emotion on his face.

A sturdy, built blonde in her early thirties bounced from the house. "Why, Hunter Dade, as I live and breathe."

"Buffy," Hunter said laconically.

Buffy Crandall, former Dallas Cowboys cheerleader and Miss Texas, according to Hunter's verbal dossier about the weekend's players. She curled a hand around Hunter's bicep like she was desperate for the warmth of hot, virile male. "Still growing, I see." Her gaze fell on Tess but skittered away without making a full assessment. "And you've grabbed yourself another fiancée. Lord in heaven, Hunter, you have *got* to slow down."

"They gotta keep up with me," Hunter said, amused. He took Tess's hand and squeezed it, sending her stomach into a flutter.

"Heard the last one got a kick to the head with a chaser of common sense on the way down the aisle, Dade." This gruff pronouncement came from a barrel-chested geriatric cowboy in jeans and plaid who swaggered over and threw his arm around Buffy.

Hunter's hand tightened in Tess's, and she could feel the strain working its way through his muscle-taut body. The humiliation and loss over what happened must be still so raw. That he was seeking comfort from the person who had dealt the harsh blow that fateful day stirred something deep inside her.

"Now, TJ, don't you be poking at Hunter," Buffy said. "He's our guest."

TJ sniffed, managing to put as much disapproval into that as was humanly possible. He and Hunter eyed each other like prizefighters deciding whether they should push each other around the ring to give the crowd their money's worth or go straight for the knockout punch.

Hunter finally said, "TJ."

"Dade."

Lovely.

"Oh, where are my manners?" Buffy finally looked Tess straight in the eye. "This must be—"

"The kick to the head," Tess said without missing a beat.

Buffy blinked owl-like. "The what now?"

"I'm the kick to the head. You know, the one that knocked some common sense into the bride." Tess curled into Hunter's side and wrapped her arm around his strong torso. "I'd had my eye on this cowboy for a while, and that day, I couldn't bear to see him make a mistake, so I stepped in."

"Did you now?" Buffy looked like she was struggling to consciously rearrange her frozen expression into something approximating an earthling. "So you knew the bride?"

"Knew her?" Tess gave her cheekiest grin, making sure she took in TJ's sour puss. "Hell, I was the maid of honor." She punctuated that with a hammy wink.

Tess and Hunter had discussed the development of their "relationship" on the flight and decided to stick with simple: he came to her show six months ago, muscled his way backstage to meet her, and *presto!* they were engaged. Raising the specter of Jenna and that fucked up wedding was not part of the plan, but TJ's mean-spirited jibe had spiked Tess's protective instincts. And if she was going to go off-script, she would do it in style.

Marta whistled, long and low. Poor Buffy looked positively scandalized.

"My motto has always been: a hard man is good to find." Tess gave Hunter's unflinching bicep a gentle squeeze, claiming it and the man for her own. "And never let the bride stand in the way of me and my hard man."

And then she popped up on her tiptoes and kissed him, a little soft, a lot heated. Pulling on his bottom lip, she willed his surrender. *Come on, baby, make it work.* Two seconds in, she felt his resistance give way, and he responded with interest.

"Oh, she'll do, Hunter Bean," said Marta, reminding Tess that they had company.

Tess drew back, but Hunter had other ideas. With a sure grip of his hand to the back of her head, he dove deep, heading for the end zone, which in Tess's case was an on-the-spot orgasm. His tongue swept across hers with a savage ferocity.

Her entire body fired in appreciation at how his strong, sensual lips took control, claiming, possessing. Owning.

Finally, he let her up for air. She supposed she had asked for that.

"Ain't she somethin'?" Hunter muttered, cupping Tess's chin and finishing off with his patented lip swipe. But he looked less than pleased. In fact, he looked like he wanted to throttle her for taking liberties with her improvised version of their origin story.

If the punishment was kisses like that, she'd be breaking every rule in Hunter's book before this weekend was over. *Adios, no-sex clause.*

"Where'd you put us?" Hunter asked, his lovingly murderous gaze still on Tess.

"In the pool house," Marta said. "Dinner'll be ready in an hour. Hope you're hungry."

"Yeah, I'm starving," Hunter said, releasing Tess to go grab their bags.

• • •

Hunter shut the door to the pool house behind him and dropped Tess's suitcase to the floor. *Fuck.* He could feel his muscles trying to break through his skin like caged wild beasts. TJ and his dig about his catastrophic wedding day had struck closer to the target than he expected. His former employer had never quite made peace with Hunter's rise to the big leagues, though every cent had been earned with blood and sweat. To be cut off at the knees by a city socialite no doubt pleased the old coot.

Tess flipping the script had been unexpected...and most

certainly not what they had discussed. 'Course, that was Tess, always improvising her way through disaster.

"Oh, this is lovely. Someone's trying to bring the ocean indoors," she said, taking in the pool house and its weird sea-faring themed décor. Was that a fucking life preserver on the wall?

She twirled, but stopped quickly at whatever she saw on his face. "Hunter, are you angry at me for changing things up? I know that wasn't the plan, but I didn't like how TJ was talking to you, and that Buffy sounds like a piece of—"

He pushed her against the door, covered her perfect body with his raging one, and kissed her quiet. The overpowering urge to take her had gripped him the moment she stepped onto the jet with her skirt swirling around her gorgeous legs. Didn't help when she got into that hissy fit about the no-sex clause. Certainly didn't help when she settled her heated sex over his and damn near seduced him on the plane. Even with all that temptation, the last straw was not that cheeky kiss she laid on him as they played the happy couple for Buffy and TJ. It was her defense of him. She had claimed him as someone worth fighting for.

No one had done that since Alison, and she had paid with her life.

Now he was kissing everything out of this woman, his woman for the weekend, because he couldn't *not* do it. Pleasure barreled through him, coating every nerve and shrieking them to rawness.

"That was not the story we agreed on," he ground out on a break to haul air. "You could have fucked this whole game up before we've even begun." And then to show her how displeased he was with her, he moved his mouth to where her swanlike neck curved into her shoulder, and marked her with a love bite.

"I'm sorry, Hunter," she moaned, not sounding sorry at all. Her raspy, pleasure-drunk voice rang against his ear in triumph. That spiked his mad and made him more determined to inflict further sensual suffering. Sure, he knew he was playing her game but damn it all to hell, he didn't care. He grasped her hands, then stretched them above her head. She groaned her disapproval and pulled away from his searching mouth.

"Let me touch you," she said, all desperation while her body beveled toward him.

"No." The word killed him to say it, but to let her have free rein would just spiral this situation out of control. Instead he rubbed his out-of-control cock against her belly. And yep, he was fully aware of the irony. Every inch of his body strained to make nice with every inch of hers. "We do this my way, princess, or not at all."

"Hunter," she gritted out. Emotions stormed over her face until finally settling on resigned but blatant desire. "Oh, God, just do it."

He restarted the sweet assault, softly, teasingly, giving them both time to work up to it. Their tongues mated, tangled, and got to know each other really fucking well. She tasted like woman, fire, all he wanted. He had never been more aroused by a kiss in his whole life.

That's when he worked his body over her soft curves. Grinding, driving himself past the edge to a place he knew threatened his disintegrating control and his mental health. He needed to stop.

Any moment now.

Cuffing her wrists with one hand, he used his free one to coast down her body and cup that curvy ass he'd been dreaming of all week. Wrong, all wrong, he pulled her closer to his erection. Locked her in tight where she belonged. They explored each other's mouths with alternately hungry and languorous attention, with not-so-gentle nibbles and life affirming sucks.

In no way satisfied, he released her arms and jerked back. Breathing hard, slumped against the door, she stared up at him through those reddish-gold lashes.

"Hunter…"

"Get ready for dinner."

A look of unbridled fury came over her face, and he stepped back. Unmanly, perhaps, but her spirit would bring out his beast if he got too close.

"That's it?"

"That's all it can be. I explained." He scrubbed a hand over his head like it might work to keep his brain matter from oozing out of his skull. "It's for your protection."

Absolutely brilliant, man.

"You can rub your body against me, kiss me like you're starving, get me good and primed, and we haven't fucked." She added air quotes to that last phrase. "That's mighty fucked up, Hunter."

His smile was inevitable. God, he loved her smart mouth. He'd love it even more wrapped around his dick, but that was impossible. He couldn't get anything out of this except her paid services as his fake fiancée. So, he'd flirted with the line—okay, trespassed in a major way—but no more. He'd ball his fists and grit his teeth and take ice-cold showers.

Then he saw it. Out of the corner of his eye, the bed

loomed like a third person in the room. The big, but not nearly big enough, bed they would be sharing.

And she saw he saw it. A naughty smile split her face before disappearing behind the blouse she peeled off over her head.

What the…?

He knew that devastating smile was still there, even though he missed it on the return when she dipped her body, showcasing that cock-raising cleavage as she stepped out of her skirt. The dick that refused to claim any part in her lips kissing and sucking it jumped like an excited puppy. *Down, fella.*

"Tess, honey, what are you doing?" *She's stripping, dummy,* his cock supplied helpfully. His IQ had already plummeted fifty points and was heading further south fast with all the blood in his brain. His gaze attached to her matching red bra and panties, a sexy contrast against all that creamy-pink skin. And don't forget the black stockings, still magically staying up on her beautiful thighs. The woman in lingerie was a sensory feast, a million times better than his fantasies.

She threw her discarded clothing on the bed and cocked her hip. "What am I doing? I'm getting ready for dinner, *honey*."

"You can't do that in the bathroom?" The one that was ten feet away. He pointed in case its location was unclear, and to give his scorched retinas sorely needed relief from all those curves.

"No, I can't, Hunter." She grabbed her suitcase and turned it on its side. Bending over, not *safely* from the knees, but like she needed to tip her toes to limber up, she unzipped her luggage. The erotically thin fabric of her panties rode up a few inches, revealing the ambrosia skin of her gorgeous ass. Between her thighs, the cleft drew his eyes to its inviting accessibility. He stifled a groan.

His cock grew thick and achy. How in the hell had he thought this would work?

Standing, she held up something. It might have been a dress or a towel or a fisherman's tarp in keeping with the damn decor. He had no fucking clue.

"What do you think for dinner? I know it's important I don't show you up." Something soft and red filled his lust-hazed vision. "With this first one, I can't wear a bra because it's backless..." She swapped it out for something dark. "...but this second one is a little low-cut. Bra or no bra?"

Think, man, think. The fate of the universe depended on the answer to this question.

"No bra." He tossed that out casual-like, as if he were one of her girlfriends, chit-chatting about what not to wear.

That drew her insolent, sexy smile. Laying the clothing on the bed, she leaned over to pluck a speck of dust off the blouse. Her heart-shaped ass tipped up, and a freckle taunted him from an unbearably hard to reach place on her inner thigh, so close to her pussy he almost collapsed with heart failure. Just upped and died on the spot.

Twisting to face him, her expression registered mock surprise. "Oh, still here? Thought you'd be hitting the bathroom for a cold shower." Her cheeky gaze made a lazy journey down his body before lingering like a kiss on his dick. Damn traitor strained taut against his zipper, itching to kiss her back.

Happily—for Jesus, there had to be a sunny side here— he noted her nipples had puckered to knobs of hard candy against the cups of her scarlet bra, silky fortresses that barely held her gorgeous tits in place. Good to know he wasn't the only one affected here.

"Careful now, Hunter. Stare any longer and you might combust on the spot." Slowly, she walked to him, still in those tempting stockings and heels that screamed sex. She placed a devilish hand against his chest, now tippety-tapping with his overworked heart.

"I know what you're thinking."

"Doubt it."

"You're thinking about the freckle hunt."

Ah, she had him there.

Stroking a finger over her left breast, she circled the freckle he had fantasized about tasting. The fantasy she was using against him right now like evidence in a court of law.

"You think you can kiss me like that and there not be serious consequences?"

"I'm used to suffering."

"I'm not as stoic as you." Molten desire lurked in the sea-glass green depths of her eyes. One of her bra straps had slipped off her shoulder, and that little moment of dishevelment jacked him up even further.

"You've got me pretty hot. You've got me wondering how good your hands would feel on me. How your cock would feel deep inside me. Last week, it wasn't enough. Clothes on like we were still in high school. Soaking my panties with your dirty talk and magic thumbs." She poked a finger against his chest. "Not enough."

She cupped her breasts and plumped them to double freaking *Fs*. "Here's one freckle, Tex." Down, down, she slowly moved her lethal hands over her ribs and her slim waist. "I have another one here." She pointed at the flare of her hip.

"And here. Hidden away." Her finger hooked the border of her lacy panties, drawing his gaze away from her perfect breasts and shapely hips to that forbidden country.

Only he was the one without a visa to travel there. Her papers were perfectly in order as that dip with her fingers demonstrated.

"Tess," he growled, not knowing if he was pleading with her to stop or go on.

She went on. Lower. *Deeper.* Glad they got that straight.

Against his chest, she splayed a hand for balance, her eyes heavy-lidded with lust, and she moved her other hand inside her panties. *Sonofabitch.* All he could do was stand there slack-jawed and let his eyes fuel his dirty thoughts. Was she anywhere near as wet as he imagined? Was she slip-sliding through her silky folds? Was she rubbing her clit until it was diamond sharp?

"Hunter," she moaned, and his name on her lips stroked his spine with how goddamn right it sounded.

Fuck, didn't she realize he was staying away for her own good? Burying his body inside hers was *the* fantasy, but getting his jollies like this—*and paying her*—was so many kinds of wrong. Loving her luscious curves with his eyes would have to be enough. Jerking off till he was sandpaper-raw would have to get him through.

"This can't happen." He pushed her against the door, more roughly than he intended. She was driving him insane. "It wouldn't be right."

Her eyes flew wide, still lust-blown, still a little bit wild. "You asked me not to touch myself until I saw you again, and then you pulled that contract crap. There was nothing in those terms about having sex with myself, Hunter. Not even *you* can stop that." Muscles loose, she slumped against the door, using it as an anchor as she stroked and stroked. Because damn it all, he was useless to her, worthless as a sidesaddle on a sow. He couldn't engage the way he wanted. Drive his cock home and feel the joy of her taking him deep. Get to know her body and what turns her on.

Apparently, touching herself while he watched with a full-on drool was one of her triggers.

Whaddya know? It was one of his, too.

The sight of her, auburn hair tumbling over her shoulders, her body undulating as she pleasured herself, that slender hand working through her slippery heat…tightened every inch of him. Gut, cock, balls.

It also toggled the switch on. He could make it good for her without indulging his own wicked wants. Help her out of this fix.

The line was fine, but then so was she.

Unclenching his balled fists, he stepped closer to heaven and sank down to his knees, ready to pay homage. In awe, he placed both hands behind her thighs and soaked up the sensations. Her silky skin, the stockings that *had* to come down, the scent of her arousal. Intoxicating, filling his nostrils with her power. Looking up, he expected to see triumph on her face, so when he found her vulnerable, he almost keeled over, or would have if he wasn't already bent in worship.

"Please," she begged, removing her fingers, still glossy from her succulent sex, to rake his hair. To mark him.

Now it was his turn to make his mark.

"I'll take care of you, honey," he whispered against the

moist spot on her panties. Softly, he kissed a freckle on the inside of one thigh, then a spot higher on the other.

Then in between.

She gave a shimmy of need, and he knew he was a goner. Any attempts at finesse went to hell in a handbasket. He yanked her panties down. Parted her with his fingers. Inhaled her like he would a fine scotch.

"You're so wet, Tess." And he was so goddamn thirsty.

Knowing this was about her and not his needs freed his mind, not from guilt, but from inhibition. Pleasure her. Love her body. These things he could do. He was built to care.

That it would fuel his fantasies for the rest of his miserable life, he'd take as a bonus.

With a gentleness he never knew he possessed, he nudged her thighs apart and licked long against her seam, savoring her. Her pussy throbbed under his attentive tongue. Thighs trembling, she gripped his hair for balance or need or just because she liked it. With each lap at her, he felt her weaken under his strong grip as she slipped farther down the door.

Getting all up in her business was a biological necessity.

But like any master of his craft, he needed room to work. When he unhinged his mouth from her body, she whimpered her disapproval, but he stayed her protests by maneuvering her to the floor. He laid her out like a buffet and took a moment's breath to admire the view. Breasts still pertly encased in that bra, panties hanging by a leg hole from her slender ankle, gorgeous legs gift-wrapped in those sexy stockings.

"Dammit, Tess, you're destroyin' me here."

"Hunter, are you— Are you stopping?" The uncertainty in her voice surprised him, that she could doubt for a moment her power over him. She looked and sounded like she might die if he didn't give this to her. No way did he want that on his already dead-weight conscience.

"Not a chance."

Hips relaxed, her thighs fell open like the curtain rising on one of her shows, displaying in full her wet, pink heaven.

Thank you, Jesus.

Bending to his enviable task, he settled his mouth into the embrace of her thighs and licked her open. She ground her hips against his hungry mouth and screamed her need. Cussin' up a storm, making him throb. There was nothing better than this, the feel of her, getting lost in her sighs and sounds.

He knew where he wanted to be. Needed to be.

His cock ached, and he skated his hand down to rub it, anything to get relief, but he checked his stroke. One touch and he'd blow his shorts for the first time since Sharon Valdez got him all hot and bothered in the gym equipment closet back in the eighth grade.

Selfish as it was, he needed to feel her when she got there, and if he couldn't bury his preferred piece of anatomy, then he'd have to go with the next best thing. He sank two fingers deep into her pliant heat, relishing the grip of her silken muscles, almost coming undone by her rising moans. The woman was loud.

He loved every second of it.

"Hunter, oh-*oh, shit*!"

Thrusting his fingers into her with a rhythmic slowness, he flicked her clit with his tongue, then applied suction to that throbbing bundle of nerves. She raised her hips off the floor and thrashed against his mouth, his name a shouted prayer on her lips as she came. Silky wetness flooded his hand. So much of it, all for him. Unable to resist, he removed his fingers and lapped up every last ounce of her pleasure like a man dying of thirst. Every little wave, sound, motion of her body, what got her there, he committed to memory. Because he hoped to make her scream his name over and over every night they were here.

Except that would not happen again. It could not.

He'd keep those memories for the lonely times, for the sleepless nights he needed a shot of relief and the only solution was his fantasy redhead playing on an erotic loop in his brain. Raising his head, he met her sated gaze.

She was panting, the swells of her still covered breasts heaving over the lace-trimmed edges. "That…that…was…"

Fucking amazing.

"Just wow," she finished thickly.

She scooted up on her elbows and rubbed a hand through his hair. Her lust-stoked pupils couldn't quite mask the gratitude he saw there and something else. Affection, which he neither wanted nor needed.

"I have condoms in my suitcase." Said with an assurance that all remaining barriers between them had been annihilated.

Standing, he swayed, dazed and drunk on this woman. Her taste still coated his mouth. He never wanted to eat or drink again.

The hard expression he knew to be on his face turned her gaze harder. "Hunter, stop being so noble."

Noble? That was a first.

"This wasn't about me, Tess." Turning away to stiffen his resolve because one more nanosecond of her lush curves would make it impossible, he headed to the bathroom, already anticipating the coldest shower in blue balls history.

How's that revenge plan working out, Dade?

Oh, faaan-fucking-tastic. I sure showed her.

"Hunter," she called after him like a siren drawing him to craggy rocks.

So tempting, but he resisted despite every muscle straining to turn and take what she offered. What was his. He leaned his forehead against the cool mirror. No help, whatsoever.

And he *still* hadn't gotten those damn stockings down.

Chapter Seven

Ding Dong! The witch is dead...

Hunter was still getting ready for dinner, not that anything could possibly improve on perfection, so Tess stepped outside the pool house to answer her phone.

"Hi, Mom," she said with fake cheer.

"Tess, did you get the invitation to my forty-fifth?"

Hi, Tess, how are you this fine evening? The forty-fifth was aspirational. It was actually her mother's fifty-third birthday party, but her white lie was so small in the grand scheme of things that Tess dutifully let it slide.

"I can't make it."

Disgust chilled the line so much Tess marveled that her fingers didn't turn to ice and detach like stalactites.

"Darling, don't tell me you're still doing that ridiculous dinner theater. You're picking up bad habits. And the audiences are the worst."

A raw welt of emotion blossomed beneath Tess's

breastbone. "No, I've quit that. I'd just prefer not to come to L.A. right now."

Her mother's sigh was heavy. Award-worthy. "Tess, surely you're old enough to move on from these childhood slights. We really must evolve in our relationship."

That burn in her chest bloomed to ravage her entire body. Every urge from her mother to "move on" was just another nick. Death by a thousand dismissive sighs.

"I'm busy with the new theater. We've got funding—"

"Where did you get it?" Deb snapped. "You haven't cashed a single one of my checks, so how are you suddenly able to do this?"

"We have a backer. A white knight," she said, unable to help the smile gathering speed and threatening to overwhelm her face. Thinking about Hunter did that, not his money.

"Darling, local theater is dead. It's New York or traveling companies. You know that."

So much for the good feels. Tess closed her eyes and forced her body to calm, praying she could retain a grip on the phone and not hurl it into the pool.

In a pause so weighty it could have crushed a semi, Tess could hear her mother building to emote. "My therapist thinks our failure to communicate stems from your wish to supplant me. She says it would be helpful if you came to a few of our sessions."

Sounded like this week, her mother had cast herself in the role of Medea, tragically wronged, forced to sacrifice her young at the altar of the gods. Who exactly would this therapy help? The frightened fifteen-year-old girl who sought out her mother's protection from Stepfather Number Four only to be accused of bewitching him like all the other new "uncles" in Mom's life? *Think you can twitch that pert ass and take him from me, Tess?*

No, the only person this therapy would benefit was the icon who needed to project an image of familial harmony as she geared up for Oscar nomination season and the inevitable Barbara Walters's *Most Fascinating People* TV special. Expecting her mother to have a come-to-Jesus moment was too much at this stage, not when the woman already thought she was an earthbound deity.

"I've got to go, Mom. I'll keep you posted about our opening night." She ended the call shaking, still confused about what her mother needed from her after all these years. Was Tess being too harsh? Deb had made irregular peace overtures over the last decade, but only when it suited her promotional needs. The first two years after Gavin came on to her had been blessedly quiet once Tess moved to Wisconsin and finished high school under Gran's wing. But a notorious paparazzo started asking questions about the perceived rift between mother and daughter, and Deb's publicist urged her mother to extend an olive branch.

Only Deb wasn't interested in making real peace. When her mother called on the day Tess started her freshman year at Northwestern, the olive branch came with thorny terms.

Forget about the past. Nothing can be gained from a walk down memory ditch. And if you must think on anything unpleasant, use it for your art.

Every day Tess lived by the lessons her mother taught her. She walled off her heart to the possibilities and kept the good stuff for the stage. Whether it was Claudette, Lysistrata, Ophelia, or Blanche, she disappeared into the part because it was easier than playing Tess McKenzie, Deborah Patton's daughter.

"You ready?" she heard in a low rumble behind her.

She turned, determined to remain unaffected no matter how— *Oh hell,* he looked so damn fine in dark jeans, cowboy boots, and a white button down, its tantalizing *V* revealing the crazily lickable hollow of his throat.

Inhaling a fortifying breath, as much to banish that conversation with Mom to the ether as to bolster herself for the night ahead—and the mess of hot male at close quarters— she activated her brightest grin.

"Just try not to screw this up, Tex."

"I swear I've never seen eyes like it. They looked right at me. Through me."

Tess inched forward on the butt-sucking leather sofa in the Crandalls' Southwestern style great room, her attention riveted by Denise, one of the weekend guests. For the last ten minutes, the woman had been slowly parsing out a story about encountering "something" in the desert, and she had *finally* reached the punch line.

"What was it?" Buffy screeched from the bar where she was blending a strawberry daiquiri.

"It looked like a lizard, but it had fur. It was a—" Denise looked left and right shiftily, and whispered, "A chupacabra."

"Bull hockey." So pronounced by the heavy set man practically sitting on top of her—John Lewis, Denise's husband, who insisted everyone call him Lew. "Blowhard" would be more apt. "It was a mangy prairie dog, Dee."

"I know what I saw." Denise shuddered and warmed

her bare shoulders with her palms. The move pushed up her breasts, which looked like two Goodyear blimps barely lassoed by scraps of fabric no wider than bandages. She slid a defiant look at her skeptical husband. "Dogs don't have spines on the outside. And those eyes."

"I believe you," Tess said, sending a sympathetic smile the woman's way.

"Don't encourage her. She's as dumb as a plank some-times," Lew spat out before lubricating his fat mouth with a slug of whiskey.

Tess parted her lips, but her fake fiancé cut off her response by gently squeezing the back of her neck. It would have rhymed with "masspole."

The moment she had walked into the Crandalls' ranch house, she knew it was going to be one of those nights. It had already been one of those days. She should have been satisfied after goading Hunter into sexy servitude, but no, a thigh-clencher of an orgasm wasn't good enough for Tess McKenzie. She could still feel Hunter's hot mouth sucking, nipping, lapping up her satisfaction. Squeezing her thighs to-gether provided not one iota of relief, but only exacerbated her frustration.

Though she had teased him about his definition of sexual relations, she truly believed that in his own oddly chivalrous way, Hunter was trying to respect her by not using her for his own gratification. *This wasn't about me,* he had said, as his blazing gaze raked over her half-naked, barely sated body. Did the gorgeous, impossible man not realize it pushed all her buttons to have a guy put her first like that?

She wondered if there was ever a time it *was* about him. Who looked after his needs, and not just the sexual ones?

Not that she was offering herself up for the job, but it sure had her thinking.

Beside her, he leaned in, the weight shift bringing her closer to him on the sofa. The man was a downright tease. "So what do you think of the rest of the cast?"

She bit off a smile: cast wasn't so far off the mark. The world she had entered was like a house party out of an Agatha Christie novel. For your consideration, ladies and gentlemen, the players.

TJ Crandall, the gruff patriarch who held court and waited a beat for everyone to laugh at his jokes, was currently showing his antique gun collection to one of the other guests.

"Our host's about what I expected," Tess said, snugging closer to Hunter to keep her conversation under wraps. Her story. Sticking to it. "Blunt, stubborn, outdoorsman. Likes the sound of his own voice. Our likely murder victim."

Hunter's mouth pulled up at the corners. "Ya think?"

"Oh, yeah. It's always the head honcho, the guy with a slew of enemies. He's welched on too many deals, probably fathered a couple of vengeful kids out of wedlock, won't give his wife an adequate shoe allowance. Hypothetically, of course."

"Of course. And what about the rest of 'em?"

Two other couples filled out the roster of weekend guests. John and Denise Lewis on one side, and on the other, Tawny and Tony Carson—their names, for real—who were weirdly cute together and finished each other's sentences.

"The Carsons are okay, Denise is a hoot, but Lewis is a chauvinistic pain in the ass who's so busy trying to get his tongue up TJ's butt he's going to do himself an injury. We'll probably find him bludgeoned by a candlestick in the library at the beginning of Act Two."

Hunter laughed so loudly Buffy shot a skewering glance in their direction. "Or mauled by Denise's chupacabra. So what does that make us in our play for the day?"

The space around her became frighteningly confined as Hunter bent his forehead to hers, the thrilling closeness filling her chest with his spicy, masculine scent. Absolute heaven.

She shot for flirty casual with a dash of Scarlet O'Hara. "Why, Mr. Dade, we are love's young dream." She smoothed her hand across his chest and fiddled with a shirt button, all things that were her right as adoring fiancée.

"And then off into the sunset?" His heated gaze fell to her mouth and lingered for half a heartbeat.

"A hundred thousand dollar sunset," she said because the intensity in his expression knocked her on her ass. "And whatever millions you make out of it."

Though he nodded his agreement, his brow puckered as if the mention of cash displeased him. Why would he set up this elaborate charade, spend time with a woman who he clearly still blamed for the worst day of his life, when there were countless parcels of land that didn't come with these strings—and countless women who would jump at a chance to be Hunter Dade's main squeeze for a weekend?

"You didn't ask what I think of the Queen Bee," she said, getting back to the teasing vibe between them.

Buffy, their beautiful hostess with a smile too wide for her face and a soap opera stare she'd used too frequently on Hunter across the dinner table. There was history between those two.

Amusement quirked his lips. "You have an opinion? What am I talking about? Of course you have an opinion."

She patted his big hand condescendingly, the perfect answer to his put down. "Yes, darling, I do, and you're looking at the mystery dinner theater expert. In our play, Buffy would be the prime suspect. With whatever poor patsy here is her lover." Holding his deep blue gaze, she tilted her head in question. "Or her former lover."

"Busted," he said easily, surprising her with his forthrightness. "A long time ago when I was young, foolish, and horny as hell. Buffy was on the downside of her Dallas Cowboys cheerleader career, and we were both on the board for a domestic violence charity."

"Domestic violence," she murmured, remembering what brought him together with Jenna whose mom was on the board of one of Chicago's most well known foundations. A million causes could have attracted a man looking to get his foot in the door with a certain well-heeled set, not to mention taking advantage of the attractive tax deductions.

"Why domestic violence?"

For a moment, she thought he hadn't heard her. Then pain clouded his eyes, and when he spoke, it was like every word took a gouge out of him. "My sister. She was three years older than me. About sixteen years ago, her boyfriend beat her so bad she died."

"Oh, Hunter. I'm so sorry." A well of emotion filled her throat, and instinctively, she placed her hand over his heart. It thumped along, finding a fast-paced rhythm with her own thundering beat. "What happened to the guy?"

"He got his," he said darkly. Whatever he saw on her face forced him to amend that bald statement. "I didn't kill him, Tess, though Lord knows I tried to."

A flush of cold followed by a wash of heat roared through her. The idea that Hunter would do violence to protect someone he loved appealed to her on a very primitive level.

"You— You tried to kill him?"

Speculative, Hunter eyed her, his gaze hooded. "All those things you said about me a year ago, how I was unrefined, a roughneck, bad news for Jenna—"

She opened her mouth to deny, but he was already there, speaking for her like a ventriloquist's trick.

"You never said it to my face, Tess, but I know you made your opinion clear to my bride. Well, you were right. I'm all that and more. I grew up in a trailer park not ten minutes from here where the kids ran in wild packs and the only law was the one of dog-eat-dog."

He brushed a loose strand of hair behind her ear. "Underneath my tailored shirts, I'm still that animal from the trailer park. You said I would have destroyed Jenna. I think what you meant is I would have degraded her by being her husband."

Shocked embarrassment curdled in her stomach at being called out for her condescension. Yes. She had thought him unsuited for Jenna and that he was *some* of those things, but that wasn't the reason for her interference. "No, Hunter, that's not what I—"

He cut her defense short with a slanted smile and brushed his lips against her ear, taking their conversation to a dangerously intimate volume level. "Don't worry, you were only doing right by your friend. And I'm not judging you for needing the special kind of loving I can give you.

There's nothing wrong with wanting it hot and dirty or getting it out of your system before your Prince Charming rides in with his trusty minivan." Cupping her neck, he threaded his long, sensuous fingers through her hair, those instruments of pleasure that had pumped her to ecstasy a few hours ago. Lust crashed through her, so inappropriate given what he had just shared. Her only choice was to hold on for the nerve-frazzling ride.

"Let's face it, Tess, you don't need to like a guy to want him to fuck all sense out of you, right?"

Her heart jerked at his sudden switch. The damage she had done when she first met him appeared to be undoable, but more crushing to her soul was that his opinion of her was as low as she felt right now. She thought they had been finding common ground, inching closer to understanding with every new intimacy, but apparently she had completely misread the signals.

Dumbfounded, she fought for balance. She needed to snap out of this fuck-daze he had her mired in. Since when had she sought Hunter Dade's good opinion?

"Dade, get your ass over here," TJ barked from the other side of the room.

"And I want to know all about you, Tess," Buffy said, grabbing her hand to pull her to the other sofa. "Let's leave the men to discuss their deals and us girls can get to know each other better."

Buffy's grip brooked no dissent. Glancing over her shoulder, Tess caught Hunter's dark stare and found herself leveled by it. Back to business and the reason she was here.

The fucking job, stupid.

Tess was blowing Hunter's mind.

It didn't help that she looked beautiful in that backless ruby dress that set off her auburn hair and draped perfectly over her cuppable, braless breasts. He'd missed his opportunity to explore them earlier when his focus had been on the moist treasure between her thighs. Notch that one up to the idiot column.

Everything about her got him hard. The sway of her hips, the curve of her lips, every word out of them. She was just so damn fuckable. Today, he had managed to keep his dick in his pants, though every second of getting her off had practically rent apart the seams of his control. Now each passing moment in her tempting presence reignited his burn for her. If that was all it was, he'd get over it. Sexual chemistry was easy to place in a box and lock up tight.

But his attraction to her had morphed into something more unsettling. He was starting to…like her. And what did an idiot do when a woman edged under his skin in that way?

What every male of the species since time immemorial had done when confronted with the object of his desire on the playground. He pulled her pigtails. God knows letting her see how affected he was by her big heart and clever smile would be too damn honest. When she'd looked at him with those soft, expressive eyes as he spilled his guts about Alison, it had enraged him.

Her sympathy loosened something in his chest, a lump of guilt and pain he held close to remind him of his true nature. He enjoyed her compassion, and he had no right to it. Best to warn her off in case she started to believe the charming shit he was shoveling and convinced herself he might have a shred of decency. Not even close. Sixteen years ago, he tried to kill a man, and Tess needed to know that the hands he would have happily used to beat Dixon Roberts into the grave were good for only two things: brawling and fucking.

Just two more nights. And then what? *Here's your money, honey, have a nice life.*

The sharp twinge in his chest acknowledged his dissatisfaction with that plan, but then none of his plans so far had played out the way he expected. That all ended now. By Sunday, he'd have what he wanted. Not Tess, at least not the way he wanted her, coming like a firecracker all over his cock, but the land. Lindo Pines, site of his childhood nightmare. And he could do anything he wanted with it.

For his mother's future and Alison's memory. So he could sleep through the night.

TJ muscled into Hunter's space, sucking up an extra share of oxygen. "You and that development outfit of yours have been making quite the name for yourselves, Dade. Though I guess with Kane's money and Cross's contacts, you were bound to do well."

It wouldn't be the first time he'd heard it. Partnering with Brody and Flynn had been as beneficial for them as it was for him, but as he had further to climb, he always looked like the Johnny-come-lately. His job was to get down in the dirt of the negotiation pit. Persuasion was a skill he'd honed with precision over the years and many's the deal he'd locked up tight even when rivals offered more money.

"I had some luck," Hunter said.

TJ nodded approvingly. He liked when the former help

knew its place.

"Got yourself a fine woman there."

Hunter looked into the arctic blues of his former employer and tamped down on the pleasure those words gave him. He hated himself for wanting that approval. Craving it. White trash upped and got himself a beautiful, classy girl.

"Yeah, she's pretty fine all right."

"Met your mama?"

"Not yet." That'd happen over his dead body, but still, his traitorous imagination wandered to putting the two of them in a room together. Introducing Tess to his mom like they were a real couple and watching Cecile's eyes fly wide at what a great catch he had made—provided her eyes weren't already lit from the gin she guzzled by the vatful. Not once had he entertained the idea of Jenna meeting her future mother-in-law. He'd not even told Cecile he was getting married, but with Tess…

Get your head out of your ass, Dade.

That impossible, unholy meeting would merely confirm everything Tess thought she knew about him. How he was mutton dressed as lamb, throwing his money around, trying to buy his way into respect and civilized society.

"Hunter, I need you." His fake fiancée's voice slid across his skin like a silky caress. "The girls have so many questions."

"We'll talk later, Dade," TJ said, in a tone that was promising.

Hunter sauntered over and lowered his body to the seat beside Tess on one of those too soft pieces of furniture, which brought her closer to him. Not that he needed the help of the sofa; she coiled her arm around his waist and snuggled in tight as a barnacle.

She tilted her beautiful green eyes up to his, showing no traces of upset with his sharpness earlier. "Hunter, everyone is dying to know how I hooked you."

Showtime.

"You tell 'em how we met?"

She blinked wide and her next words came out in a breathy Marilyn gush. "Should I or would you rather…?"

He stroked his fingers down the ladder of her spine, absorbing her shiver as his gift.

"You tell it, Tess." Anticipation at how she would handle it thrummed through him.

"Well…" Her tongue darted over her lips and, surprise, surprise, his jeans became uncomfortably tight. "Just over a year ago, I was acting in a show, and my old college roommate brought her fiancé, this handsome hunk here, to see it."

"You mean he was engaged to someone else when you met?" Tawny asked incredulously at the same time Buffy snapped, "You're an actress?"

"Yes and yes," Tess replied smoothly. "Of course, I had no idea to do anything… After all, he was with one of my closest friends, and I'd never betray that trust. Hunter and I had a fight that first night we met." She sighed wistfully. "He hated me."

"Hate is such a strong word," Hunter said, feeling warm at the memory. "And it was more of a healthy discussion."

"Okay, an argument. You see, Hunter didn't much like the play because it's about *female power* and *sexual agency*, and it offended his Neanderthal notions of what women can and can't do."

He couldn't help his smile or the way his dick bucked

like a bronco at her pointed jibe. "That play was about women using sex as a weapon, Tess. Of course, I'm not gonna approve."

She walked impossibly slender fingers along his thigh, the third one adorned with his ring. Foreign satisfaction warmed his chest at the sight of his brand.

"We ladies have to use what we can when you men are being so stubborn." Her sweet smile was a fake, but damn if his body knew the difference, especially when her hand moved higher on his inner thigh. Not squeezing or applying any pressure, just hovering with wicked intent.

"So you're an actress," Tawny said. "Would I have seen you in anything?"

Just tonight's spellbinding performance, Hunter thought wryly.

Tess gave a cool smile. "No, I work mostly on the stage. That's where my heart lies."

"It certainly doesn't lie with your friendships, seeing as how you broke up his wedding to a woman you supposedly called a friend," Buffy announced with rancor.

An uncomfortable look passed over Tess's face, and he opened his mouth to defend her because she was his woman. But he needn't have worried because his woman was a pro.

Staring right at him, she held the moment for a perfectly exquisite beat. "I knew she couldn't make him happy."

His heart punched hard against his rib cage at how sincere that sounded. *She's acting, idiot.* Happiness had never entered the equation where Jenna was concerned. Happiness didn't get you respect or power or put you in a position to bring the hammer down on a deal. Happiness wouldn't bring Alison back or stop his mother's self-destructive behavior. It was so fucking abstract that the possibilities of the word had never once entered his mind.

But right here with Tess, that alien feeling crept inside his blood and bones. Settled and made itself at home. Pulse on a dangerous uptick, he did the one thing he should not do. He kissed his fake fiancée because in that moment, she made him happy.

Happiness might be abstract, but this kiss couldn't make the same claim. It was so full-blooded and real he wondered how he had survived without it all these years. Without her. He slipped his fingers down to the base of her spine, the backless dress giving him unrestricted access. Tess shifted against him, enough to allow his hand to palm the rise of her perfect, pert ass.

No panties. *Fuck.*

"Lord in heaven, Hunter, let her breathe," Buffy said shrilly.

Reluctantly, he unlocked his lips, but before he dragged his mouth away completely, she rubbed her nose against his. A little unexpected tenderness that turned his heart to mush and his cock to granite in one devastating swoop.

Tess's opaque gaze cleared and was replaced by something more challenging.

"And the proposal was perfect."

The proposal? Shit, the proposal. With Jenna, he had taken her to the Signature Room on the ninety-fifth floor of the Hancock, a traditional place for romantic dates and the unveiling of engagement rings. Soft music, so-so food, a stunning view of the city: all calculated accessories to the perfect popping of the question. Sliding his ring on Tess's finger ten seconds before they arrived at the ranch had been the opposite of romantic.

Funnily, it had felt a hundred times more real.

The ladies leaned forward in expectation. "Tell us about the proposal!" Denise chirped. "I love a good proposal story."

"Yes, do tell, honey," Tess murmured, the little minx.

A few seconds ticked over while Hunter scrambled for a likely tale. It would have to be something unique, something worthy of this special woman. His neurons untangled for a brief, illuminating moment.

"Tess is on her feet a lot with this latest show of hers, so she's rather partial to foot rubs."

"While eating ice cream," Tess added, quick as a whip. "Ladies, you haven't lived until you have your man rubbing your feet while you eat ice cream."

"Sounds like heaven," Tawny said, a hint of green in both her skin tone and voice.

"So we were on the sofa at home, just our usual. Foot rubs, ice cream, chatting about our day," Hunter went on, warming to the tale while his palm heated on the silky soft skin of Tess's ass. A flash fantasy of their "usual" becoming a reality tried to take hold, but he shoved it deep into his brain's attic. "And I slipped the ring on her pinky toe."

He looked into Tess's eyes, seeking approval. The catch in her throat and the bloom on her cheeks were his answer. Relief flooded his veins at pleasing her. Raising her left hand, she rocked the perfect Home Shopping Network move with her fingertips on his chest, displaying the sapphire engagement ring to perfection.

Atta girl.

"I asked her if she'd be okay with me giving her foot rubs for the rest of her days and—"

"I took another bite of Phish Food first." Tess sounded a tad breathless. "For strength, and well, no life-changing decision should be made without the benefit of ice cream. Amirite, ladies?"

The ladies nodded in awe, even the usually skeptical Buffy who hung on every single word. Christ, they were knocking this out of the park.

"Hunter had already eaten all the chocolate fish, so I had to have a serious think about whether I was prepared to spend my life with someone who steals the best part. But…" She paused, her eyes filled with warmth and love. Hell and damn, she was something else. "I decided he'd already stolen my heart and soul. And I deserved those foot rubs."

Her flirty smile kicked his libido into overdrive and sent his palm deeper to cup the perfect globe of her ass. In retaliation, she skated her hand perilously close to where his thigh met his crotch. His dick reacted like the circus had come to town.

"Well, ain't that a kick to the head?" Buffy asked. "Don't you think so, TJ?"

"Sure, sure, sweetheart," TJ muttered distractedly, his focus on his guns.

The conversation turned to nonsense Hunter paid no mind to. All he could think of was getting Tess back to the pool house to take what was rightfully his. That contract was as dumb as he was when he drafted it, and nothing was going to stop his cock from finishing what his tongue had started earlier.

Brushing his lips against her ear, he gave the woman her due. "Nice job."

"Figured I owed you for this afternoon," she whispered,

keeping their conversation out of earshot of the other guests who had wandered off to freshen their drinks. "One good turn deserves another."

Gently, he squeezed her ass cheek. "You trying to kill me with the no-panties thing?"

"I would have thought your self-control is so strong it shouldn't affect you in the slightest. Man of steel, it seems." Creeping up from where she'd settled against his neck, she laid her tempting lips close to his ear. "You ever heard of Chekhov's gun, Hunter?"

"Nope."

"It's a principle we apply in the theater. If you put a gun on the stage in Act One, you'd better make sure it goes off by Act Three."

Turning his head slightly, he smiled against her temple, loving that little patch of soft skin he encountered. "You're going to have to explain its application to our particular situation."

"What it means is that you started this a week ago in Chicago. You loaded the gun, waved it about—"

"Are we still talking about the gun?"

Her look was cutting. "Waved it about, and then expected us to pretend it's not there between us. Instead you make a unilateral decision not to use the gun. When it's already on the stage. Ready to go off."

As usual, she was right, and very soon, for want of a better metaphor, his gun would be going off inside her slick, tight sheath. But disagreeing with her was too much fun. "I'm not seeing how you can complain, Tess. As it stands, you've got two orgasms to my zero. Most women would be pretty stoked with that scorecard."

"I'm not most women. I'd rather this was mutually satisfying."

Holy shit, this woman would never stop surprising him. Even after he had tried to scare her off with his tales of his mangled past, after he'd tried to humiliate her, she was still here. Breaking down his barriers, picking him apart.

"Tess, what I said earlier—"

"About how women like me enjoy slumming it with a bit of rough, and how I don't need to like you to want your special kind of loving?"

She uttered it with a practiced coolness, but his mama didn't raise no fool. He had hurt her, and while that had been his intention, his self-perception as trash was his problem, not hers. He opened his mouth to say so, but she had more.

"You were right, Hunter," she whispered, her eyes filled with emotion that clenched his heart. "I said awful things back when I didn't know you because I thought you were all wrong for my friend, and with my fancy education and my love of Greek classics, I assumed I was better than you. So if loving how you make me feel now makes me a hypocrite…" She tried to smile, but it looked like it might do her an injury. "Sue me."

Stunned couldn't begin to describe what he felt right now. 'Course, she meant how he turned her on, not anything more. But still. Her raw sincerity toppled him.

"I'm sorry I was such a jerk, Tess. This place… It gets to me, and I took it out on you." He grazed his lips across her temple, inhaling her unique scent deep so he could store it for another day. "Frenemies again?"

She laughed softly, a perfect whisper of breath against his jaw, and tipped her face up to his. "Frenemies forever."

In the span of a few heartbeats while they held each other's gaze, the air heaved with terrifying significance.

"It was wrong of me to cut you out of the no-sex decision, Tess. I've been trying to respect you" — *and punish myself* — "and that wasn't very respectful."

"Thanks, Hunter," she whispered thickly. "I appreciate that."

"That's not my only regret about my behavior today," he murmured, needing to get this back to the sizzling sexual chemistry between them. The stuff he could handle.

Her lips twitched. "Now, Hunter, I think we've established you behaved like a gentleman."

Only Tess would think his denial of self-pleasure was in any way gentlemanly. "Yeah, I was all politeness when I fingered you good and made you scream my name. And my chivalry reached new heights when I licked the sweetness between your thighs while you shuddered against my mouth."

A raspy sound escaped her throat. *Gotcha.* She closed her eyes, and her feathery red-gold eyelashes spread like delicate fans on her cheeks. Above the rim of her wine glass, Tawny Carson sent a curious look their way, then turned back to her phone.

"I'm sorry for a host of other things," he continued in her ear. "Such as not kissing that tempting freckle on your breast. Not feeling the imprint of your pretty pink nipples on my tongue." He bit her earlobe, a tender puncture that drew her husky whimper. "Not coming all over your beautiful tits." This was crazy, but she made him this way. His barely-leashed control was about to unravel, and priming the pump with a little honest dirty talk would make the moment he sank deep into her all the sweeter. "And in about two minutes, I'm going to take you back to the pool house and show you exactly how much I regret not fucking the living daylights out of you."

"Oh, I know where I've seen you," Tawny cut in. "Tony, I know where I've seen her."

She held up her phone, the screen facing out and showing a photo of two women in a restaurant, one of them with similar red hair to Tess. It looked like one of those long-distance telephoto images that spies shoot.

"You're that actress's daughter," Tawny continued.

Tess's body went as stiff as laundry on a South Pole clothesline. A look of—was that fear?—marred her face. "I'm an actress," she said softly, like she needed convincing.

"Yeah, but aren't you her daughter? The one who won the Oscar for…"

"*Convent Rules*," Tony finished for his wife.

"About the nun who falls in love with…

"The archbishop."

"Deborah Patton!" the Carsons screeched together.

"What?" Hunter asked stupidly, staring flabbergasted at his fake fiancée. *Deborah Patton?* He might be outside the loop on most popular culture, but even he had heard of Deborah Patton. That could not be right. Tess was her… daughter?

Panic flared in Tess's eyes. If the floor was to split at the seams and drag her to hell, Hunter imagined she might be fairly happy with that outcome. Conversation ground to a halt as everyone turned their way.

"Why, Hunter, I'm guessing from that look this is news to you," Buffy said in a sing-song voice. She wagged a finger. "A couple holding secrets is not a good way to start a marriage."

The temptation to jump into the awkward pause and

claim he'd known all along flitted across his rusty brain, but the damage was already done. How in the hell was he supposed to convince TJ that he was in a real relationship with Tess when he didn't even know who her mother was? And would it have killed Jenna to mention it?

"So, Tess, we want to hear all the gory deets about Deborah Patton," Tawny said, picking up the conversational slack, which was about the only thing loose in the room now fraught with tension.

"She's just Mom," Tess said, her tone strained. *Just my famous mom who I can't be bothered to mention to the man I supposedly love.*

"She's so talented," Denise gushed. "One of my favorite actresses of all time. What was it like growing up with her? Did you meet her dishy leading men? Did you get to visit her on set all the time?"

Tess froze in his arms, plain seized up like a slab of cool marble. "She traveled a lot, so it was easier for me to stay home because of school." Her eyes slid to Hunter's, something on the spectrum of disappointment in their green pool depths.

"And you're in Chicago instead of L.A.?" Buffy asked. "Mom not able to get you an audition for the latest *Transformers* movie?"

That earned Buffy a sharp look from Tess, a spirited response that was more like the woman he knew. "I'm not interested in using my mother's reputation to get ahead."

The group continued to pepper Tess with questions, every one of which she answered patiently and mechanically. But he could feel her rising discomfort, like she was waiting for a sword to fall. Didn't take long.

"Wasn't there some trouble a while back?" Tawny asked. "Something about her husband running off with her money?"

A fiery blush crept up Tess's neck to her cheeks, and her thigh trembled. He tightened his grip, that crazy need to protect her from all comers pounding through his blood, despite the fact that right this minute, she needed saving from *him*.

"Yeah, about ten years ago," she muttered.

"That must have crushed your mom," Tawny went on, oblivious to Tess's distress. "To trust somebody like that—"

"Who's only using you for your cash," Tony supplied helpfully.

"The poor woman," Denise said, clasping Tess's hand in sympathy. "Thank God she had you around to comfort her."

Still stiff, Tess smiled thinly, and her shining eyes found his. He felt like they were having a whole conversation here, and because of his useless Y chromosome, he had lost the codebook. Something had happened to her; that revealing ringtone and all that stuff about not wanting a relationship and her mom's "new jerk in tow" were pieces of a more complicated puzzle. Unfortunately, any sympathy he had for her predicament warred with seriously more negative emotions: anger, humiliation, and he-was-downright-fucked.

Standing, he pulled Tess with him and close against his body. Her skin had turned to ice.

Buffy narrowed her eyes. "Looks like you two have a lot to talk about."

He nodded to a hard-faced TJ, swept the room with his gaze. Fury blinded him to anything but a host of judgmental blobs and prevented the usual pleasantries. Sliding an arm around Tess's waist, he walked her out of the room.

Chapter Eight

Fuck me.

Hunter steered her forcefully to the kitchen, the shortest route to the pool house, tension singing in an operatic screech from his body. So she had kept this itsy bitsy piece of information back, but who knew Tawny would recognize her? It had been years since Tess had been seen in public with her famous mom, and even then, she was an awkward teenager in shapeless tees, desperately trying to hide the curves her mother despised.

It was a toss-up as to which was more depressing: that Hunter was about to chew her out or that somehow her appearance was so unchanged that a perfect stranger could pick her out of nowhere.

At the kitchen's back door, she halted. "Hunter, I'm sorry."

He angled his hand around her jaw and placed a thumb over her lips, killing cold the effusive apology she planned.

She gasped at his touch—gentle, forceful, and arousing as hell.

"Don't. Fucking. Speak."

"Let me explain."

"Get your sweet ass back to the pool house. We're not doing this here."

Anger surged to sensitize her skin. Did he think she was some chippy he could order around because he happened to sign the checks?

"Now, wait a minute. You can't talk—"

The ground flew from beneath her feet, and for a split second, she worried her heels had gotten the best of her again. But no. She had been upended by a caveman and thrown over his shoulder like a deer carcass from the day's hunt.

Can't. Even.

"Hunter, put me down at once."

He ignored her. Admittedly, it had been a long shot.

With lengthy, purposeful strides, he exited the kitchen and rounded the pool to where they were staying. Pounding her weak womanly fists on his back seemed a touch too dramatic, and heaven knows she wouldn't want to be accused of being dramatic.

Hunter threw open the door in a rather manly fashion, pushed inside and dumped her on the bed, a move so sexy that her inner slut drooled. Oh, who was she kidding? After this afternoon, there was nothing "inner" about it. Add in a spot of furious man pacing, accompanied by equally furious hair raking, and this had the makings of a knock-down, heart-pounding, no-holds-barred fight.

The sex was going to be spectacular.

"Tess, don't you think our year long relationship might have been enough time for me to find out your mother is one of the most famous people on the planet?"

"Yes, but—"

"Yes, but what? It looks like I don't know you from a hole in the wall."

She lifted her shoulder in a half-shrug. "Well, you don't."

"Because you chose not to share it," he said, exasperated. "Not just an omission but a lie. You said she was a schoolteacher."

When Hunter had asked about her upbringing before, she'd kept it close to her chest with a tale of middle class nirvana—father dead when she was a teen, raised by a schoolteacher mom. It wasn't a *complete* lie.

"She played one on camera."

He looked heavenward for inspiration. Finding nothing, he zeroed his steely gaze back on her. "And your father? Is he dead or is that a lie as well?"

She sat up on the bed, propelled by her heart thudding like a wild beast fighting to escape her chest. "He could be. I don't know."

"What does that mean?"

"It means, I don't know. I have no idea who my father is or was. My mother used a sperm donor."

That put a hitch in his mantrum and turned those midnight blues to compassionate pools. So not her intent. She wanted to fight but only on her terms. Where the wounds could be shored up quickly and painlessly.

"You're shittin' me."

"She has a Queen Elizabeth complex. She didn't want to submit to a man, but she especially didn't want a man to have rights over me. I was to be 100 percent hers." Creating a clone of Deborah Patton was her mother's plan. And who needed a flesh-and-blood father when a dose of baby batter and a test tube fulfilled the job admirably? A child was just one more fashionable accessory for Mom, a fad she bored of as soon as the paparazzi flashes faded.

Hunter shoved his hands in his pockets and shifted uncomfortably. "Hell, I didn't know my father, either."

Tess's eyes shot up to meet his. "Really?"

"Neither did my mama. Just another anonymous fuck behind a bar in Caden, Texas."

Any self-pity she might have been harboring vaporized with that shocking statement. The life this man had led: a sister he was ready to kill for, a trailer park backdrop that spurred him to fight for wealth and respect. Hunter Dade toppled her.

He sat beside her, his elbows on his knees. They were quiet for a few not uncomfortable moments—before he opened his mouth and ruined it.

"Don't this beat all?" he asked, his tone one of bitter amusement. "Trailer trash engaged to a Hollywood princess. Seems I can't stay away from you rich, society girls looking for a little fun in the dirt."

That stung. Her childhood had been filled with the best schools, the swankiest parties, the most fashionable vacation spots, usually in the company of one of her mother's lackeys. It had been a lonely way to grow up, but she could see how it might look to an outsider. One more poor little rich girl playing at real life with the assurance her safety net would kick in when she needed it.

"Money isn't everything, Hunter."

His upper lip curled. "But it sure as hell helps. Looks like you're not hurtin', either, given your living situation."

Right, her living situation. Hunter thought that temporary house-sitting gig in the lap of luxury was her normal instead of the rat hole she could hardly make rent on. It wasn't her job to disabuse him. Let him think whatever he needed to keep afloat his righteous indignation at society.

When she refused to take the bait, he tried another tack. "So tell me about your mom."

"Nothing to tell," she said cautiously. "We're not close."

"How come? She not like your boyfriends?"

"I didn't like hers," she snapped and immediately felt him stiffen beside her. *Clever boy.* He'd set it up, and she'd walked right into it. Wishing she could bite that back, she turned away and picked at a loose thread on the bedspread.

He cupped her jaw and directed her back to face him. His dark eyes narrowed, honing in on her with a focus that burned her alive. Seeking weaknesses. If he kept it up—if she let him—she would not make it off the island.

"Why didn't you like her boyfriends?"

"They were jerks. Assholes who were using my mother for what she could give them."

"Uh-huh. What else?"

Ignoring his insistence, she stood, but he snagged her wrist gently and pulled her down on his lap.

"Hunter," she muttered ineffectually, powerless to resist cuddling closer to him. With his long torso, she fit in perfectly against the crook of his neck. Breathing him in like her well-being depended on it, she let his scent filter into her nostrils and smoke through her blood.

He rubbed her thigh in long, sensuous strokes that

spelled comfort as much as sexual promise. Her skin was itchily sensitive. Her nipples had been in a state of permanent arousal all night and were now as hard as bullets, desperate for the salve of his blunt hands. How could she be so turned on at this most inappropriate time?

"What happened, Tess?"

"Nothing." Even now it seemed foolish and not worthy of a ten-year grudge. Just your standard pulp novel plot of stepdaddy getting a little too friendly with his teenage stepdaughter. Nothing illegal had occurred, and it hadn't screwed her up. She had a healthy attitude to sex—witness her sexy shenanigans on this very floor earlier. As long as no one wanted to get serious, she enjoyed the attention of men.

Which is why this three-day fling-in-the-making was perfect for her. Except the part of undiluted sex god was now being played by Mr. Sensitivity.

"You can talk to me, you know," he said, still stroking her thigh with a potent brew of possessiveness and strength.

If she breathed a word of this to Hunter, he would get angry like he had with that scum who killed his sister. And because there was no dragon for him to slay, he would throw a metaphorical cape over her bare shoulders and carry her home. There was something unquestionably honorable about this man, an old-fashioned protectiveness that fisted Tess's heart. Tell him about a guy who had wronged her years ago, and he'd want to punch somebody—and then hold her.

Such kindness might kill her.

"Hunter, I'm sorry I didn't reveal my super-secret identity. I should have told you, but it's been so long since anyone recognized me that it never occurred to me that it was important." She clambered off him to a stand, rolling the fatigue from her shoulders. "I'm going to take a shower. If you need to go back to Southfork for damage control, I understand."

Moodily, he regarded her with barely disguised disdain. He didn't like that she wouldn't open up. Hell, *she* didn't like it, but it had worked like a charm for years, and it would take more than Hunter Dade's dark-eyed disapproval to make her turn tattletale.

As she turned away to the bathroom, she heard a grunt of male discontent, followed by a word she could not believe had spilled from his mouth.

She whirled around. "What did you call me?"

"I called you a coward."

"I— I am not!"

He lifted an eyebrow. "You're exhibiting the classic symptoms of avoidance."

"Wow, Hunter, sounds like you've been digging into the lady mags."

"Gotta read somethin' while I'm gettin' my hair cut."

Don't smile. Don't show weakness.

Straightening to her full five-feet-four, she sent a triple shot of titanium to her spine. "Earlier you said something about winning being the best therapy. Well, for me it's the stage. That's where I let it all out."

A flickering flame of a smile brightened his face. "I know. That first night I saw you in that lousy show, you were a woman unleashed." He stood and crowded her against the dresser. "Just like when you came against my mouth. And honey, it was a privilege to be part of both experiences."

Her heart went thunkity-thunk and made an all stops crash around her chest.

"But channeling your emotions into Shakespeare don't make the problems go away. What happened with this guy, your mom's husband? I felt how you reacted when Tawny brought him up. You were shaking like a beach shack during a hurricane."

Emotion thickened like syrup in her throat. "Nothing. He was just another dick," she said, reluctantly slipping from his enticing grip and into the bathroom. She wasn't even mad at Gavin anymore, though if she was truly honest with herself—a rarity when she was off stage—she'd acknowledge that her miserable relationship record *might* stem from her stepdaddy issues. Or her mommy issues.

Call Lifetime. I've got your movie of the week right here.

Before she could register it, Hunter had pushed her back against the vanity and got all up in her personal space. Though the way Hunter did it, it was no longer her space. He invaded, occupied, possessed with the sheer force of his presence. Hemming her in with both hands on either side, he dipped his forehead to hers.

"So is this our argument for the day?" A low, sexy rumble in his throat. "Because you're not playin' your part, princess."

"Maybe I think you play dirty." Getting personal was definitely playing dirty.

His smile was brief, no longer comforting. "Where is this jerk now? The one who ran off with your mom's money?"

"Why do you want to know?"

"Because I think he hurt you, and I'd like to hurt him."

Her breath trapped in her lungs. Yes. Yes, she'd like that.

No. Just as quickly, Miss Independence drew up the drawbridge. For so long she'd relied on her inner resources that the idea of letting someone else take the wheel terrified her.

"Rest assured, Hunter Dade, standing before you is one of those self-rescuing princesses. I'm not your..." She stopped short, clamping down on the end of the sentence.

Hunter's eyes flashed. "You're not my sister. I get that, but there's nothing wrong with asking for what you need."

In his eyes, she saw compassion and assurance that he would make it better. He had been making it better the moment he re-crashed into her life, and every second with him increased her need to threatening proportions. Strong arms made to hold her, words calculated to soothe and comfort.

Ignoring it had been her coping strategy for years. Her mom refused to meet her halfway, so Tess retreated to a deep place and only came out when the role required it. Sometimes she thought she imagined it, created a memory of Gavin grabbing her hand in that laundry room and inviting her to say hello to his little friend. Other times, she dreamed that her mom had taken her into her arms and told her it would be okay. She'd take care of it, and no one would hurt her ever again.

But wishful thinking got her nowhere. It had not happened like that. No fairy-tale ending, no mom to hold her, no hero to save her.

Back at the ranch, Hunter had tried to scare her off about his past and the beast inside him, but she knew better. Crude, blunt strokes were not this man's weapons. He was a needler, a poker, a guy who knew how to apply the right amount of psychological pressure to get his victim to cooperate, confess, or capitulate. It was incredibly seductive. And very, very dangerous.

He smiled, warm and wicked. She thumped him in his exceptionally resistant chest.

Those navy eyes widened as big as saucers. "That's more like it, baby. Let it all out."

The man must have shares in Infuriating Asshole, Inc. "There's nothing to let out, you dolt. Stop trying to get me mad."

"Can I help it if I like it when you are? You know it turns me on." He wedged his hard body between her quivering thighs, stamping on her belly the fullness behind his zipper. "Trying to get me to back off here is like hollering down a well."

"There's nothing in our agreement about offloading our baggage."

"Funny how convenient that contract is when it suits you. Shit getting a little real, huh?"

"Certainly feels real." She twitched her hips against his burgeoning arousal. What she needed was a night out of her head where she could lose herself in the sweet bliss she knew only this man could offer. Despite the obvious danger to her heart, subsuming her body in the oblivion of his was all she could think of. She spread her palms over his hard chest, absorbing all that vitality beneath his shirt. Hoarding it for long, lonely nights in her hovel.

Gripping her wrists, he pinned her tight to the vanity. "That sex as a weapon thing can only get you so far, Tess."

Wanna bet? "I'm not damaged, cowboy. I don't have hang-ups about my body, I don't use sex to mask my problems"—*much*—"and right now, if you don't touch me in some very hot, very wet places, I might die." Actually, she'd make sure she got off a couple of right hooks first, and then she would drop dead from desire. "That's what I need from you, Hunter. No more talking, just a whole lot of doing."

Annoyance, maybe more, flashed on his face at her blatant attempts to shut down the inquisition. *Boo hoo.* Last she'd checked, filthy fling rules were pretty clear on the subject of sharing-and-caring.

It was just not done.

"Well, if there's one thing I'm good at, it's a whole lot of doin'." His smile was half wry, half pissed. All wolf. "Let's get you fucked."

Chapter Nine

What was it about this woman that turned Hunter into a raging beast who would track, maim, and kill anyone who hurt her? He'd known that night he had reconnected with her that there was trouble ahead. And now it was confirmed by everything she refused to say. He wanted to fuck her, possess her, save her— And then he wanted to spend every second of his sorry life making hers better.

Not that Princess Tess wanted any kind of TLC that didn't involve his hands, tongue, and dick loving every inch of her. She'd made it clear. Shut up and do her. Take her to some place she didn't know existed before she met him. And he would. He would take care of her the only way he knew outside of throwing a punch or writing a check.

He nudged his knee against hers and then slipped his thigh between her legs. Right at the spot where he knew she needed soothing so badly. Across the crest of her breasts, he ran the backs of his fingers, absorbed the warmth of her skin.

Luxuriating in the feel of her, he increased his attentions tenfold with his hands all over her curves and dips. He might be a roughneck who didn't know a Monet from a Picasso, but he recognized beauty when he saw it. And right this second, he convinced himself that every inch of her belonged to him, if only for the next few hours.

"Hunter," she said breathlessly. Knowing how much he affected her did it for him right there. She nibbled on the corner of his mouth, licked the seam of his lips. He parted to let her in, and they kissed each other long and deep, just two people enjoying the hell out of each other.

He cupped her ass and lifted her flush, and she ground her tight, sexy body against him. Like she needed the connection as much as he did.

Like she needed it to exist.

She placed her palms on his chest and ran wild over his pecs, up to his shoulders, down to his waist, across his hips. *This is mine,* she would think. *And this. And don't forget this, it's one of my favorites.* A foolish fantasy perhaps, but then this was his night to be a fool.

She was still ridiculously covered up, and he knew he'd have to do something about that soon. First, he planned to enjoy the flashes of skin he had exposed so far. Unveil her like a gift, take his time. He moved down her throat and settled his lips at the top of her breasts.

"Hunter," she gasped. "Hunter, Hunter."

Taking her moans as orders, he ground his erection against her. His mouth covered her breast through the sensually thin material of her skimpy dress. With his teeth, he dragged the fabric aside and took her rosy nipple into his mouth. Nipped and suckled, licked and tasted.

She coasted a hand between their bodies and cupped his cock.

He groaned.

Perfection times heaven.

Knowing his control was slipping, he removed her hand and held it behind her, then grabbed the other when she tried to stroke him again. "Not yet, honey. I won't last if I let you have your way."

She growled her frustration and he chuckled, twisting her so she faced the bathroom mirror. The evidence of his need dug into her spine. The evidence of hers shone back in her reflection. Pupils lust-blown, nipple puckered like a ripe berry, mouth slack with desire. Blotches of pink skin bloomed across her throat and chest, a trail of brands from his mouth.

"Please, Hunter. Don't leave me like this."

Half dressed, one breast exposed, she looked glorious. Making her beg for his rough touch was supposed to be some sort of victory, but that's not how he felt. Sex had never been about forging a connection before, but with Tess, with this woman who needed what only he could give her, a whole new world had opened up. This felt like how it was supposed to be between two people, joined body and soul.

"How do you want to come?" He raised the hem of her dress and trailed rough fingers down the cleft of her world-class ass. "You want me to get my tongue all up in your delicious heat?"

Whimpering at his words, she met his gaze in the mirror with a heavy-lidded one of her own. She tried to say something, but only a moan came out.

"Or do you want my fingers stroking you? Making you

wet?" He dipped a finger into her already soaking pussy, drawing another raspy moan. "Wetter? Stretching you to get you ready for my cock?"

Her knees collapsed, but his arm around her waist kept her afloat.

"I'll take that as a vote for fingers."

Seeming to gasp for the air to speak, she finally managed, "No."

He froze. Shit, he'd pushed her too far, let his beast come out to play. "I'm sorry, Tess. I shouldn't speak to you like that. I know you're not that kind of girl."

Those green eyes went wide. "No, I am. I'm exactly that kind of girl. I love your dirty mouth, Hunter Dade, and you can use it on me anytime." Turning, she palmed his erection, which expanded under her firm touch.

How the hell could it not?

"Fingers or tongue won't be enough. I need this inside me now, Hunter. All of you. No more selfless orgasm gifting, no more altruistic holding back your pleasure. This is for both of us, baby."

A sweetly uncomfortable fullness ruled his chest, and with a heartfelt groan, he claimed her mouth. His whole life of pleasure and pain was conveyed in the seal of his lips and the thrust of his tongue.

What had this woman done to him?

Hunter's reaction at what should be something so fundamental—mutual sexual fulfillment—moved her in a way she would never have thought possible. He really didn't expect generosity from his bedmates. Didn't think he deserved it.

And the kiss he laid on her? This must be what it was like to be kissed by someone else's soul.

She grasped at the buttons of his shirt, and he helpfully shucked it. Next, the jeans dropped with a speed that belied his usual slow 'n steady movements, though she wouldn't have been surprised if he'd had to tug on them awhile given the resistance of his immense erection. Inhaling a lungful of desire-charged oxygen, she took a blessed moment to appreciate what Texas had created.

There was no good reason why this man should ever wear a shirt again because he was nothing short of spectacular. Shoulders to rival Captain America, a chest so broad she'd need a map, an eight pack that had to be illegal. His sexy hip indents looked like the perfect trail for her adventurous tongue. And the destination of her pleasure hike? That long, thick cock, purple veined, epically engorged, and fully erect for her.

Come to—no, for—*me.*

"My eyes are up here, honey," he said in mock sexy affront.

Dragging her gaze away from all that hard magnificence killed her a little, but the reward quickly compensated. Hot, dark desire lurked in his eyes.

He foraged in his toiletry bag, perched on the bathroom vanity, and extracted a three-pack of condoms. She could be a smart-ass about it and mention those best laid plans not to get laid this weekend, but she figured she'd already pushed her luck.

With a deliberate slowness, he fisted that most impressive example of male perfection and stroked in that way a man did, rough and mean. A bead of pre-come leaked from the bulging tip and her mouth watered in sympathy.

Oh, my.

Deftly he rolled the rubber on, his gaze glued on her, those eyes seeking to uncover all her secrets.

"Bed?" he grunted.

She shook her head and pushed down her dress, relishing the slinky slide to her ankles. His sharp intake of breath made all the sensitive area between her legs go soft. Or softer.

"Tess, you are fucking beautiful." There was awe in his voice and a reverence in his expression that grabbed her heart hard. No one had ever looked at her like that, like she mattered more than anything. It stole her breath clean away.

He moved in, establishing a skin-to-skin connection. "It's just you and me here. No audience, no critics, no contract, no business deals. Got it?"

She nodded dumbly, not sure what she was agreeing to. Sex, yes. But that request—*order*—encompassed so much more. It required her to drop more than her dress to the floor.

His flagrant erection nudged her belly. Well, more like it demanded every iota of her attention. With no trouble at all, he lifted her onto the vanity so they were perfectly aligned. Angling her thighs wider, he hooked his arm beneath her knee to expose her further to his penetrating gaze.

"Use your fingers to get your sweet pussy ready for me."

Fire raced to her cheeks at those provocative words, amazing considering the raw, heated sensations already doing a number on every cell in her body. When she touched herself before to incite him to pleasure her, she had drawn on something different. Someone different. The sexy siren as stand-in for women everywhere, wielding female power over a man. Lysistrata, Medea, every goddess who fell for a mortal, every mortal who fell for a god. Not that she had been faking her reaction, but it had started out as a role and turned into so much more.

What was happening now was no fake. She was out on the wire, letting him see all of her.

Using two fingers, she did as he ordered. Those wild navy eyes latched on to her busy fingers. "That's my girl. Keep rubbing but don't come yet. I need you good and wet for me because I'm big and I don't want to hurt you."

"I can take you," she said, spiking her words with challenge. "I'm so ready for...it." *It?* What was she, twelve? Dirty talk was the one area she couldn't act her way through.

His lips twitched at her hesitation. "For what? You want this?" Ever the tease, he rubbed his cock against her swollen folds and made introductions.

Hunter's cock, meet Tess's pussy. Thrilled to make your acquaintance.

"I need you. So bad." She tried to sound sultry to match the words, anything to counter how exposed she felt, but it barely escaped her throat on a desperate puff of air.

"Use my name. When I fuck you, I want you clear on who's filling you up good."

"Hunter, I need you"—she panted—"in me."

"Say the words. The real words. Tell me what you need."

The man was absolutely infuriating. "I need you to—"

"What, Tess?"

"God*damn* it, Hunter, I need you to fu—*ohh!*"

One hard, fluid thrust and he was inside her at last.

Holy Channy Taytay, the man put the awe in awesome. He stayed in place, just held still, letting her adjust to his size and absorb the changes flowing through her body.

"Good?" she asked him, half-statement, half-question. Good couldn't begin to describe how it felt to be on the receiving end of Hunter's immense gifts, but she'd like the confirmation from him.

He slid out. "You don't even have to ask, Tess. You're so tight—" He lodged himself inside her again, an expression of pleasure-pain on his face. This time, his thrust was deeper, more powerful, and was accompanied by a chest-filling groan. The sensation of fullness, better than any feeling she had ever had, was heightened by the expanding emotion in her chest.

"I knew you'd be tight and hot, but this is un-fucking-real."

He set up a sensuous rhythm of slow, consuming strokes, every one building to something extraordinary. As if the pleasure wasn't already too much, his mouth found hers and offered hot tongue-sweeping kisses to match those deepening thrusts, all while one hand cupped her thigh and held her in place for their joint pleasure.

And joint it was. Locked together, all parts of their bodies rubbing and sliding, sucking and fucking. The electrifying connection coiled her tight and tore everything loose.

"Touch yourself, Tess," he demanded. "Like you did before."

Taking orders didn't usually do it for her, but then she'd never had a boss like Hunter. She moved her hand to her pulsing clit and stroked it gently. Then a little harder because that's how she liked it.

"More, Hunter. Please. I need more."

She needed to forget her troubles and lose herself in him, but every move deep inside kept her anchored in the present. Both his hands gripped under her thighs, keeping them wide to guarantee the deepest reach as he thrust into her hard, relentlessly, and to the root. She held on to his shoulder and let her other hand work her spot.

Telltale tingles heralded the pleasure shockwave. It corkscrewed down her spine and pooled low in her belly. Fingers flying over her clit, she tried to hold on to each shivering vibration as it grabbed hold and pulled taut on every nerve ending. Through her explosion, he stroked long and deep, longer and deeper, imprinting his cock inside her.

Imprinting him.

"Fuck, you feel so good, Tess."

He was close. She sank her nails into his back, loving how he arched into her, like he was trying to climb inside her. Her nail-grab also had the effect of raising his head from where it was buried in her neck and focusing his full attention.

Not her purpose at all, because now their gazes were locked in the most intimate way. As Hunter had so eloquently pointed out earlier: shit was getting a little real.

She wanted to look away because it had never been like this. Might never be again. Shoving that disturbing thought deep and then shoving the reasons why she might be disturbed by it even deeper, she let the power of her orgasm take hold.

And then as if she didn't have enough problems with all the heart-stopping Hunter eye-fucking, he slowed his stroke to a steady, slow rhythm. Age-old, yet frighteningly new. The man was holding back, prolonging this moment and making sure she would never forget him.

No fair, but then he'd never played it that way.

"You feel me, Tess?"

Of course I feel you. Your rock hard cock is all up in me. But that wasn't what he meant. The man was a straight talker, a shoot from the hip kind of guy, and he was giving her something special here. Demanding that she match his intensity with her own.

He was never not negotiating.

She swallowed against a desert dry throat.

"Tell me, Tess."

"I feel you, Hunter." Too damn much.

"Good, because no woman does it for me like you do. You've got me all twisted up." Holding her in place, he slammed into her hard again and again. Another long, consuming thrust pushed her on the rickety rollercoaster toward a second blinding orgasm. "No. One."

Those words—heartfelt, perfect, Hunter's—sent that pleasure coaster crashing off the precipice. He followed her over with a final pump of release and a loud roar, through the other side into this strange new world where nothing would ever be the same again.

Chapter Ten

"Mornin', Marta."

Hunter dropped a kiss on the tiny woman's forehead and grabbed a cup for the coffee brewing in its usual spot on the kitchen counter.

"You're drippin' water on my floor, Hunter Bean." Clucking, she threw a dish towel at him that was barely big enough to mop a fingernail of spilled coffee, never mind the moisture he'd picked up from his swim. Satisfied she'd made her point, she went back to flipping pancakes like the ones he used to wolf down by the dozen.

As a kid, he'd eaten more home-cooked meals here in three months than he'd had during his fifteen years with Cecile. Despite waiting tables in a diner, his mama never got the cooking bug, so it was either figure his way around a microwave or starve. Marta had shown him a third option, and every day after putting in his ten hours on the ranch, he came into this kitchen and learned how to feed himself properly. He had to, since Alison had died.

Before his world came crashing down, his sister used to make pancakes with a mix, humming a pop tune as she whisked and cooked. They were nowhere near as good as Marta's, which were made from scratch and came with organic Vermont syrup instead of the generic store brand that tasted like gloopy liquid sugar. His sister didn't cook breakfast often, mostly because Cecile hated anyone making noise when she was hung over. But one morning stuck out. Cecile was over at her gentleman friend's, and they had free rein.

"What happened to your eye?" Hunter had asked his sister the minute he walked into the trailer's small galley kitchen. The purple bruise looked so sore it made him wince to rest his gaze on it.

"Just me being dumb," Ali'd said. "If my brains were ink, I wouldn't know how to dot an *i*."

Red flags popped up in Hunter's head because that wasn't something she usually said. That was one of Dixon's favorite phrases when he called her stupid. They'd be sitting on the sofa watching TV and he'd tell her she was dumber than a post or a bag of hair or something else colorful to let her know she meant nothing to him. Just some bitch who should put up or shut up.

Dixon had tried to take Hunter under his wing, like the prick needed a little brother to mold, anything to prop himself up. *Hunter, women are like tiles,* he said, *you lay 'em right the first time, they let you walk all over 'em for life.* Whenever Hunter called Dixon out for his disrespect, he got a look of such hate from the guy that Ali usually had to distract the fucker with a big wet kiss or a hand on his crotch. She'd saved Hunter's ass a million times with her ability to smooth things over. Right until the end, she protected him.

That morning in the trailer, he'd asked the question he dreaded putting to her. "Did Dixon do that?" Her boyfriend was a grade *A* asshole with a nasty mouth, but Hunter would never have thought he'd graduate to hurting a woman physically. "Did he hit you, Ali?"

"No!" Too quick. Too defensive. "I just tripped on the stupid step getting into this dump. Now eat your pancakes."

And he did, with extra margarine and generic syrup. They had tasted like morsels of heaven and did a fine job of displacing his anxiety about his sister getting pounded into mincemeat by her boyfriend.

Two weeks later, she was dead.

One day after that, so was Dixon.

Marta's chatter pulled him back to the present as she filled him in on so-and-so and this-and-that in that easy way of hers. He half listened, but his mind had wandered back to the warm bed and warmer woman he had left not thirty minutes before.

Tess had been hurt by her mom's douchebag husband, and before the day was out, he'd have the whole story. The mere thought of anyone laying a hand on her, with or without her permission, had Hunter's ribs squeezing all the air out of his lungs. How had it come to this—with him looking to protect the woman responsible for his humiliation in that church a year back?

That plan to bring her down a notch? Make her regret sticking her beautiful nose in? It didn't seem like such a good one now. Might have been the worst plan ever because hurting her would be like hurting a part of himself. In just over a week, she'd managed to insinuate herself so far beneath his skin that removing her would require a boatload of anesthetic and a sharp knife.

Last night Hunter had tried to hold back, trying to make it good for her, trying to keep it locked on the pleasure. But with every pump of his blood-gorged cock into her slick-for-him heat, his heart had answered with a double-timed beat. *Feel her. Protect her.* Maybe more. Pointless, but hell if he could stop his brain from wandering down that thorn-bordered path.

Speaking of places his mind was averse to visiting... TJ strode in and raised two bushy eyebrows when he saw Hunter leaning in against the counter.

"It's like I've traveled back in time, Dade. You in my kitchen, botherin' my staff, like you've never left."

"He ain't botherin' me, you old fart," Marta said, slapping TJ's hand away from the plate of bacon. "That's for guests." TJ scoffed and eyed Hunter like he had memorized every last piece of silver and the former help better not get ideas.

"Any chance we can talk soon?" Hunter asked, the fires of determination burning strong again. In all the lust-haze, he had almost forgotten why he was here. Not to get laid or make eyes with his fake fiancée—or not only that. The true mission.

"Make me an offer," TJ gruffed out.

"Six-five."

Wry amusement quirked the old coot's lips. "Never thought you had it in you," he said as if Hunter's offer of six point five million dollars was chump change. "That day I picked you out of that bunch of delinquents at the trailer park, I expected you'd work here for a couple hours, get bored, steal something, and go back to running with your crew. Probably end up in prison or worse like that punk who killed your sister. But every day, you showed up here like clockwork, ready to get your hands dirty and learn a trade. You could say I saved your life, Dade."

Rage boiled up in Hunter's veins. The only person who got him out of Lindo Pines was Hunter Dade. If it hadn't been TJ's beneficence, it would have been something else. Oil rigs, construction, sketchy work on the edge of illegal to get him started. He would have done anything to escape and a backbreaking job offer from the man who owned the trailer park was as good as any.

"You want to hit me now, don't you, Dade? I can see it in your eyes, that itch to knock me flat. You're still that white trash hoodlum with a falling down drunk mama and a chip on your shoulder big enough to muscle the competition out of the way. You might have money, but you got no class. And your green will only get you so far with that woman of yours."

Anger clogged Hunter's throat, and his fists balled under his folded arms. He couldn't shake off the boiling emotion, because TJ was right. About all of it.

What kind of madness was this? Hunter was loco for a girl who had culture, education, and breeding in spades, but also sported the added pedigree of bona fide Hollywood princess. Within five seconds of meeting him, Tess had spotted him as bad news for Jenna. She saw he didn't have the resources to make a woman like that happy. Any woman, including Tess.

Slow clap for you, Dade.

Pushing aside the heart-wrenching conclusions, he refocused on what he needed to do.

"If you think so poorly of me, why'd you invite me to visit?"

"Curiosity, mostly. Always interested to see how my former employees are gettin' along. And I needed to see how much you wanted Lindo Pines." He paused, sizing Hunter up so he could find more ways to cut him down. "That dog won't hunt. You're gonna have to do better than six-five, Dade."

The buzzing sound would not shut up.

Tess pried open one uncooperative eyelid and got her bearings. The anchor on the wall. The life preserver she might need before the weekend was through. Ames.

Or Amy's smiling face on Tess's phone screen, which disappeared to "missed call" because Tess was notoriously slow in the morning and Amy should know better. She lowered her head to the pillow and took stock.

No Hunter, but his spot beside her was warm and the air was spiced. Vaguely, she recalled him whispering plans for a swim and that she needed her rest for what he planned to do to her later. Wicked, delicious things.

Last night had been the most amazing night of her life. Better than her first standing *O*. Better than her mention in the "Actors to Watch" column of the *Chicago Tribune*'s theater section. Though the no-sex clause of the contract had failed to pass muster, Hunter had been adamant about following the rest of the terms to the letter. After the bathroom vanity sex, she got her foot rub, they had a quick argument about *Alien* versus *Aliens* (Hunter actually thought the sequel was better, which she pointed out were grounds for breaking off their fake engagement), and then they topped it off with more mind-melting, glorious, down and dirty loving.

Hunter had been so caring, every stroke of his hands designed to pull double duty of torture and cherish. What he had done, not just the off the charts sex, but being so present in that rock solid way of his— It had reached a part of her she had boarded up years ago when her mother stopped being a mom. Naked therapy for the win.

The phone buzzed again, and Amy's toothy grin cut into her sensual memories. Girl was persistent.

"Hey," Tess said on answering. The ungodly hour made her voice sound extra croaky. Scratch that. Screaming Hunter's name as she came again and again had made her hoarse. Orgasm hoarseness. That was a new one.

"Why are you whispering?" Amy asked loudly. "Are you in church?"

"It's Saturday."

Amy snorted. "Yeah, but don't they have those mega churches everywhere in Texas? With coffee shops and beauty salons and pastors cracking wise? I'd be going every day."

"Nice stereotyping," Tess snapped defensively. So what if she would have tossed off something similarly patronizing less than twenty-four hours ago. Spending time in close quarters with a man who refused to conform to her misguided pre-conceptions had made her rather fond of the Lone Star State. And one of its more handsome denizens.

"So how's Hunter?" Amy asked, the epitome of coy. "You get lucky yet?"

Not quite ready to go there, she invited her old pal, deflection, to the party. "Did you guys check out the theater on Bryn Mawr?" The crew had been tasked with researching possible theater front spaces on Chicago's North Side.

"Yeah, Marcus said it smells like eight-day old tacos. Sort of specific, but whatever. I figure a coat of paint will work wonders." She gave a naughty giggle. "I can't believe we're so close, and all you had to do was sell your body."

Tess blinked rapidly. "That's not what this is."

"Mmm, a dirty weekend with a big payout. Sure sounds like it, though it doesn't look like it would be a hardship. The guy is smokin'."

"Which you know because…?"

"He stopped by the theater before Thursday's show."

"What?"

Amy chuckled, pleased with the effect her words had. "He was looking for Derek. They had a private conversation in the dressing room, and when they came out, our not-so-benevolent overlord looked like he'd crapped his pants. No visible injuries, but I bet it's really hard to get shit stains out of leather."

Tess's heart trip-hammered against her rib cage as she remembered Hunter's words about trying to kill his sister's boyfriend. *He got his.* Hearing he had dealt with Derek, likely threatened him, and he hadn't breathed a word, sent her brain into a tailspin.

"You could've given me a heads up, Ames."

"I didn't know it was him until I did a little Google-Fu on your fling this morning and put two and two together." She tutted. "You dirty, dirty girl. You never said he was that hot. I can see why you laid waste to that wedding, bitch."

"That's not why. He was all wrong for Jenna."

But even before the words had found air, guilt flooded

her chest, canceling out the thrill of knowing Hunter had defended her. The bride might have had a Jimmy Choo-clad hoof halfway out of the church vestibule, but Tess had practically kicked her out the door. She thought she was doing the right thing in validating her friend's doubts, especially when her friend professed her love for someone else, and it had all worked out, hadn't it? Jenna was happily engaged to Steve who admittedly was just dullabolical. The poster boy for Argyle sweater vests, he had once spent an entire evening regaling Tess about his hunt for a rare stamp from Sierra Leone.

He was still looking.

But different strokes, right?

Last night while she and Hunter recounted to their rapt audience how they met and fell in fake love, she had joked about stealing him from under her friend's nose. But what if her tricky subconscious had a co-starring role? Could she have played anti-Cupid because she wanted Hunter Dade all to herself? Maybe her friend would have gotten over the fur baby lover and learned to love Hunter the way he deserved. Who wouldn't be crazy about the guy after spending time with him? He was funny, sexy, built, and great with his hands and tongue.

And possibly still in love with Jenna. So he said he'd moved on, but the mere mention of her name seemed to change those dark eyes to the color of regret. Here she was throwing herself at a guy who was likely hung up over another woman, and Tess was the reason why they were no longer together.

That was so. Messed. Up.

"I've got to go," she said to Amy, desperate to finish

this conversation that had exploded at the hands of a truth grenade. "Say hi to the guys for me."

"Will do. And keep up the good work. We're proud of ya!" Tess could almost hear her friend's knowing wink on the other end of the line. *Click.*

Stepping outside the cottage twenty minutes later, Tess took a deep breath of the surprisingly warm October air, seeking some measure of calm. In the shower, she had tried to wash away the angst she felt after Amy's dig about putting a halt to *The Hunter and Jenna Show*, but it clung to her skin like a tequila sweat hangover. Two facts were unassailable.

She had broken up her friend's wedding.

She was falling for the same friend's fiancé.

And she was having a hard time figuring out which came first. Had she seen her chance to steal her heart's unconscious desire when Jenna confided her doubts about marrying Hunter?

No. She refused to believe that. Jenna needed that extra push to escape her parents' hold and fall headlong into the arms of Steve, the guy she was really in love with. But just because her friend felt nothing for Hunter didn't discount Hunter's feelings for his former fiancée—his *real* fiancée. If his heart was still jonesing for Jenna, was there room in there for Tess?

Cool yo jets, girl. Talk about overcrowding her mental real estate— It'd only been a week since he'd shown up at the theater. She closed her eyes and inhaled a lungful of clean Texas air. Didn't help in the slightest. Deep breathing was so overrated.

Her gaze dipped to the paving stones at the side of the pool and the large, wet footprints that trailed a path to the main house. Texas Yeti or Hunter Dade? A smile tugged at her lips at the thought of a slick, gleaming Hunter hauling his multi-muscled form out of the pool and padding indoors like a sleek cat. As she approached the back entrance to the ranch, Hunter's voice carried out from the kitchen, loud and clear.

"Marta, you're too good to me. You know those frittata things are my favorites."

A clucking noise indicated Marta approved. "So this girl of yours seems really nice, Hunter Bean."

"She feels real nice. In my hands." An "Ow!" punctuated that. Marta must have thumped him for his insolence. Nice job, Marta.

"You gonna take her to see your mama?"

A few moments ticked by, the tension palpable all the way out to the patio. Finally, Hunter spoke in a voice so melancholy Tess's heart cracked. "Cecile's not fit for seeing anybody, Marta."

"And you think this plan of yours is gonna fix her? You know she ain't been right since Alison died."

"Long before that," Hunter said firmly. "But I'm going to do what needs to be done. Getting her out of there is just the start."

Marta clucked again. "She don't want to be fixed. Some people are meant to be that way."

"I don't believe that," Hunter said, no give in his voice. "Nothing's set in stone."

Realizing that if Tess stayed out here and eavesdropped any longer her ears might sizzle and fall off, she walked in. "Morning all, I could murder a cup of—"

The words stalled in her throat. Hunter stood at the

stove, stirring eggs and looking good enough to lick all over. His broad back rippled as he worked the food, the muscles moving like cogs under his silken skin. Respectful, hot when dry or wet, a defender of vulnerable women… And he could cook.

Dayum. The maximum concentration of sexiness allowed by law.

As he turned, she caught traces of discomfort in his expression, but he quickly covered it with a gorgeous grin. "Hey, honey, you hungry?"

Unlike her usual propensity to spout without checking in with her brain first, her graveled cavewoman response remained all in her head. He slid the frying pan off the burner, skirted the counter, and gathered her in his arms.

"Hunter, you're wet," she muttered obviously.

"Drippin' all over my floor," Marta mumbled in solidarity.

His lips moved to Tess's ear and nibbled on her sensitive lobe. "Guess I need to work on gettin' you all caught up."

No need, already there. Another pair of panties ruined.

She splayed both hands on his chest to push him away, but the strength seemed to have fled her arms and legs. Thank God he was holding her up. Just as that thought formed, he slipped his large palms to cup her ass and stroked it lovingly.

"I meant to come back to ravish you again, but I got put to work here like the old days." He rubbed her nose with his. "We okay?"

She nodded, suddenly shy around him. Peeking up, she tried not to look in his eyes directly. Like gazing on Medusa, nothing good could come of a prolonged visit to those swirly depths.

"I'm going to be busy with TJ later, but maybe we can go

horseback riding after breakfast," he said, still cradling her ass like he owned it, which in truth he did.

Horses? She shuddered. "Me and four-legged beasts don't really mix."

"You did just fine last night with a two-legged one. And after lunch, the ladies are talking about heading into town for…" He tipped his head back, giving her a prime view of the tanned column of his throat. She wanted to sink her teeth into it and plant her flag. "What are they going into town for, Marta?"

"Ginger and green tea detoxifyin' seaweed wraps."

Hunter made a face like a little kid faced with porridge when he expected Cocoa Puffs. "Now, don't that sound appetizing?"

Tess let loose a laugh that relaxed her nerves some. "It's a spa treatment, Hunter. A way to get your skin all smooth." It also happened to be really expensive and beyond her usual beautifying budget. A bottle of Dove body wash was more her speed. She'd take it out of the hundred thousand dollars she had coming to her.

"A spa treatment, huh? Well, Caden's sure come up in the world if we're offering spa treatments that sound like fancy sandwiches."

Caden. Where Hunter said his mother had conceived him with the help of an anonymous behind-the-bar rendezvous. He had been talking about her before Tess walked in, so likely, she still lived in the area.

"If you have family to visit, then don't let me stop you. Or maybe I could come with." Anything to avoid climbing a beast the size of a woolly mammoth or hanging with Buffy and the girls while they pumped her for information on her famous mother.

Expressive eyebrow pop ahoy. "You been listenin' in, Tess?"

"No— I mean, I *may* have heard a mention of your mom…" Heat flushed her cheeks at being caught with her ear to the wall. "Is she okay?"

He squinted at her, gunfighter style. "You remember that call I got last week when I was over at your place?"

The one that led to him dropping her like burning coal after he had rocked her world? It rang a bell. She nodded.

"I had to come back here to see her. She can't really look out for herself, so I'm trying to do it for her."

"I'm sorry. Is she ill?"

He gusted a long sigh that caught at her heart. "She's an alcoholic, and sometimes she gets into trouble. Hurts herself. She won't ask for my help, so her neighbor calls when something happens."

Aww. The thought of a big, strapping alpha male with a weakness for his mom liquefied her internal organs. Hunter had dropped everything, even foregoing a sure thing with Tess that night, to go see his mother because she needed him. *Getting her out of there is just the start.* Did that cryptic statement have something to do with why they were here this weekend? This property he was buying?

"She's lucky to have you."

"Don't know about that, but I keep trying. I come from a long line of stubborn, and my mama's the worst."

"Mothers," she scoffed. "I hear you."

He chuckled. "Careful, honey, you might find we've got stuff in common."

"We wouldn't want that. Not when our differences are

so much more interesting." As well as enough to get her all worked up.

"Oh, I don't know. As much as I enjoy the differences, particularly the anatomical ones, being on the same page can be just as hot, don't you think?"

Her heart and lungs contracted, and the frazzled thoughts in her brain spun out like bowling pins. She dipped her eyelids to his blockbuster chest and imagined they weren't just on the same page, but in the same apartment, room, bed. The same life. Listening to his comforting drawl while cradled safely in his arms might be her newest version of heaven. That was the first time a man had found his way into her dreams instead of her nightmares.

He had "talked" to Director Derek.

Evidently scared the living crap out of him from the sounds of it, and more amazing, he had kept it to himself and hadn't used it to score man points with Tess. Instead, he had pulled off the Holy Grail of Evolved Male: he read a woman's mind, figured out something was wrong, and fixed it.

It'd been so long since she had anyone in her corner, apart from Gran who she missed more each day instead of less. And while she had no need for a protector, Hunter's actions reached inside and touched a cold, closed part of her. She was starting to like him—a lot—and not just the dirty talkin' protective version. She liked when his voice went buttery soft at the mention of his mom.

Argh! Why was her mind even going there? Her hormones were supposed to be the brains of this outfit.

With great reluctance, she slipped from his grip and grabbed a cup of coffee. Wordlessly, Marta passed a plate laden with a veggie-studded frittata to her.

Tess smiled her thanks as she picked up a fork, realizing she was ravenous. "So, Marta, I have some burning questions about Hunter." She cut off a corner of the omelet with her fork and slid it between her lips. Eggs, the most perfect food. Bananas could take a running jump.

"Marta, don't let Tess bully you into revealing my deep dark secrets." Hunter leaned his elbows on the counter, a move that made his shoulders appear as broad as a bull's.

Tess shot a withering glance at Hunter, letting him know she would not be denied in her quest for information. And maybe because she was annoyed at how much those shoulders affected her girl parts and how much the man affected her elsewhere. "How come you call him 'Hunter Bean'?"

Marta huffed out a laugh and eyed Hunter with that maternal gaze again. "On account of him being as skinny as a bean pole when he first came to work here. Only fourteen and he was as thin as store-bought thread. Nothing like how he turned out."

If that wasn't an invitation to look, she'd jump in on that therapy action with the momster. He flashed a rogue's grin, and her stomach got caught up in a swoop.

"Yeah, he turned out okay," Tess murmured, boosting his smile wider and her heart higher. *Grrr.* "So how did he get all those muscles?"

"Throwing bales of hay around, building barns. He's always liked building stuff. Knew he'd go far with that."

Hunter flashed an aw-shucks smile. "Stop talking about me like I'm not here."

"You know, during all our dates and conversations on the sofa"—she grinned sweet enough to cause diabetes, reminding him and Tess this was fake, *all of it*—"you never told me why you went into property development."

He stabbed a pepper in her frittata, and she dueled with his fork adorably when he went in a second time. Stop that cuteness right now.

"Growing up poor in Texas with not much in the way of schooling doesn't leave a lot of choices that don't lead to a heap load of trouble or keep you lower than dirt. If you want to make money fast and honest, then it's either construction or oil. I prefer looking up to the stars to digging a hole."

He finished with that lethal Dade smile. Holy wow, it lit him from inside and lit something inside her. *Looking up to the stars.* She liked the sound of that, all the optimism it held. And she had thought the no-sex, Buffy-glaring, fake-engagement weekend would be the hard part. Foolish girl. Pretending she wasn't bowled over when Hunter Dade smiled at her with a grin that seemed tailor-made for her, that was problem numero uno.

Pretty funny for someone who claimed faking it was her life.

Chapter Eleven

Try as he might, Hunter could not keep from grinning as he led McArthur out of the stable.

"I'm not really the outdoorsy type," Tess muttered for something like the twenty-seventh time while kicking at the dirt with her cute red cowboy boots. Brand new ones, too, by the looks of it.

"You don't need to do anything. I'll be in charge." He took her hand and placed it on the saddle horn, mighty amused at her hesitancy. Tough girl Tess afraid of a gentle giant like McArthur? "Now, just pop your foot into that there stirrup and let me take care of the rest."

Five seconds later, she was seated in the saddle with a helpful ass push-slash-grope. Ten seconds after that, he had snugged in behind her, his thighs cradling and holding her in place.

She peeked down with a slight turn of her head, her pretty brow puckered with concern. "It's awfully high up.

Shouldn't we be wearing some sort of protection?"

"Got plenty of protection in my pocket, and old McArthur here is as steady as they come. He won't buck as long as you let him do his thing and don't get hysterical. He can sense fear."

"So squeeze my flop sweat back into my pores."

"Exactly."

After a couple of minutes at a slow trot, Tess's body language had eased up as she relaxed into his embrace. They continued like that for a while, okay with being quiet. He wasn't a restful person by nature, but a strange peace settled over him in this moment.

"Would've thought you'd know how to ride a horse, Tess. Don't you Hollywood princesses know your way around a pony?"

Her sigh was more amused than annoyed at his poke. "No time for that. My mother wanted me to focus on performance, dance, and voice. What I'd need to become an actress."

"But it's what *you* wanted? Acting?" Maybe she'd been stage-managed into this life, though he couldn't imagine Tess doing a damn thing if it didn't please her.

"Not when I was younger. I wanted nothing to do with it, but then I got to college and something changed. The minute I stepped onto the stage at Northwestern, I knew it was where I was supposed to be. Changed my major the next day."

Her obvious joy in that infected him, and he curved his lips against her neck. There was nothing better than finding what you were meant to do. Or who you were meant to do it with.

"And the world's a better place for it. You're one hell of an actress."

"Liar," she said with no heat.

"So maybe I don't hold much truck with some of your material, but you, Tess—all that fire and spirit—you are a vision to behold. Both on and off the stage."

He meant it. That night he'd first seen her on stage in that Greek play about women withholding their loving to force their men not to go to war he'd been riveted to her presence on the stage. That glow of hers was like a campfire he wanted to warm his hands on. Truth be told, the inappropriate attraction he'd felt, and denied, might have had something to do with why he'd insulted the play. He'd been intimidated by her self-possession and unsettled by his draw to someone so clearly out of bounds.

They continued on in silence, the *clop-clop* a poor comfort to the see-saw of revelatory emotions inside him.

After a few moments, he spoke again. "So, has your mom seen you act?"

"No, she's so busy—"

"And you don't talk to her much anyway. Because of Gavin Jansen."

She stiffened in the saddle, her muscles locking up like cement was struggling through her veins. "H-how do you know that name?"

"Not hard to find out." He'd called Brody after breakfast and had him run a background check. Deborah Patton's fourth husband, out of six, was currently a fugitive from justice, wanted on charges of embezzlement and fraud.

"Talk to me, Tess," he soothed in her ear. "It's just me and old McArthur here. Both of us are real good listeners.

You and I might not be much to each other, but I can be a friend."

Whatever she needed, he would give it to her. A shoulder to cry on, a pillow to lie on, a patron for her dream. The differences between them were too damning for anything more lasting, he knew that, but if he could improve her lot in any way, he would. Knowing her life was better, even without him in it, would be happiness of a kind.

Her breaths started to come in shallow draws, her distress a palpable thing.

"I'm here."

She made a sound of frustration low in her throat, an acknowledgment that she was tired of fighting him and he'd worn her down. "I— I was fifteen when they got married, and every day for the first two months, I could feel his eyes on me whenever I walked into the room. Following me around, grasping with his gaze. I hated it."

Jesus. What a dick. But Hunter had a sneaking suspicion that this piece of shit didn't draw the line at ogling his underage stepdaughter.

"One day, he cornered me in the laundry room and asked me for help sorting colors from whites. This involved him taking out his penis."

"Fuck."

"Well, he wanted to." A maniacal, watery giggle escaped her throat. "I managed to slip by him, got the hell out of there, and headed to the set of Mom's movie."

He could feel that throbbing vein in his temple kicking up, the one Flynn told him looked like a stroke in waiting. "So your mom went ballistic?"

"She called me a dirty liar."

The words hissed out of her like a deflating balloon. "She didn't ask him. Just said I was jealous of the time she spent with him—which I was. She had that right."

Hunter put a brake on the horse, cupped Tess's chin, and directed her to face him.

Her eyes were soft and shiny. "I moved out that day and went to live with my grandmother in Wisconsin. Gavin was also my mom's financial advisor. A month later, he embezzled a fortune and ran off to Bali with a makeup artist. Still there as far as I know."

"No extradition," Hunter said in a voice so strained he barely recognized it in himself. Fucker was smart, heading for a country with no agreement. Not that that would be a barrier to Hunter's brand of justice. "There are ways."

She held his gaze, assessing him closely, a cloud of confusion on her face.

"Say the word. One of my partners is ex-Special Forces, the other one's a nerdy computer whiz."

She gaped. "Thanks, but it happened a long time ago."

A stray thought struck him. "If the guy turned out to be such an obvious dickwad, stealing money and all, how come your mother didn't come around?"

"It's easier for my mom to believe a guy would steal from her instead of making the moves on her fifteen-year-old daughter. The first is a breach of trust, and it could happen to anyone, the second is humiliating for her. It was like…"

"You'd become a rival," he finished.

That clarification seemed to bring on a new rush of emotion. Her eyes welled, making him doubt this plan of his to draw her out.

"She blamed me for why he left. I caused trouble, rocked

the boat. Now she wants to make it up to me with money, but I can't—" The ending choked in her throat.

"You can't forgive her."

She nodded. "I needed her to be my mom, and instead, she acted like I'd stolen something from her. Her youth, her potential. It had always been lonely as her daughter—I practically raised myself—but only then did I realize I couldn't rely on her anymore."

He knew that feeling, the isolation of realizing you had only yourself to depend upon. After Alison died and Cecile cut him out of her life, he'd figured out that one person, and one person alone, would be his salvation. He was the dictionary definition of "self-made man," but hell, it would have been nice to know his mama was still there for him the way he was trying to come through for her.

Recognizing that emotion in Tess should have been comforting, but instead it just sharpened his pain at what he couldn't have. This connection between them was worth exploring, except she didn't want to explore it with him. She'd made it clear last night what his function was this weekend.

Tune her up good and keep the chat to a minimum.

She faced forward again and settled back against his chest with a deep breath. "I heard you visited the theater, Hunter. Talked with my ex-director."

His grip tightened on the reins in memory. "He won't be botherin' you or any of the ladies there again." Telling the sniveling little prick that Hunter would stuff his nuts down his throat and make him a steer if he didn't change his ways seemed to do the trick. Hunter congratulated himself on the hefty dose of restraint he'd employed.

"Thanks for that, Hunter. And thanks for listening."

"Anytime, Tess."

But "anytime" was a pledge he couldn't keep, and they knew it. She shifted in the saddle, pushing her butt against the erection he sported permanently around her.

"You wanna go there, Miss McKenzie?" Probably not her exact intention, but he figured he'd make it easy for her to transition back to what this weekend was about: financial goals and hedonistic pleasure.

In her nervy giggle, he heard her relief that they were leaving the serious topics behind. "No idea what you're talking about."

"Take the reins."

"What? I can't!"

"Sure you can. Just hold them and let him have his head. He starts to go too fast, pull back. We're heading toward those trees, and he knows the way."

Tentatively, she did as she was told, holding the reins loosely as he instructed. He worked his hand under her jean skirt, pulled her panties aside, and found her wet and waiting for him.

"God, I love how you're always ready for me." One finger worried her clit, and he imagined the throb between her thighs was like an extension of her heart, a pulse that beat specially for him.

"Faster, Hunter. I need it faster."

"Trust me, Tess. You'll like what I've got in mind."

Alternating between deep plunges inside her and a rough abrasion of her clit, he kept her hovering on the edge of pleasure. His hips rolled forward, dancing to the beat of his blood, and he allowed himself this moment to get lost in her, in this fantasy of being the only person who could fulfill her every need.

"I have to come," she begged. "Please let me come."

"Soon. And then I'm going to take you into those trees and fuck you so hard you're going to need that spa treatment to recover."

With one last sensuous swipe through her swollen folds, he abandoned his torturous attentions and grabbed hold of the reins.

"C'mon, boy!" Hunter kicked and sent the horse into a gallop. The abrupt motion thrust her forward against the saddle's swell, a move he knew would create the perfect sensual friction between her legs and trigger her climax. She screamed her release, and his only regret—the only one he would acknowledge right now—was that he wasn't inside her when she came.

Soon he would be, so he rode faster toward the trees.

"Chupacabra!"

Tess watched as her new BFFs knocked back shots of tequila, punctuated with face-scrunching slices of lime. She had agreed to be the designated driver, which was clearly a mistake because if anyone needed an adult beverage, it was her. The detoxifying seaweed wrap might have helped relax the taut muscles still aching from the most sensuously energetic sex of her life, but really it was the maddening muscle in her chest that was the big-ass problem.

She was falling for Hunter Dade, and tonight she needed a distraction.

From the worn leather booth where the girls had been

seated by Rowdy, their server, Tess drank in the Silver Dollar Bar located on the main street in Caden, Texas. Horseshoes, Stetsons, and antique farm equipment hung from the ceiling. Looked like a lawsuit in the making. The mechanical bull in the corner was already attracting a healthy crowd. No live music, but the country music cranking out of the speakers was tempting a few people to flirt with the edges of the dance floor.

A gen-u-ine spit-and-sawdust honky-tonk.

Above the rim of her glass of ginger ale, she assessed her new crew. The girls had dressed up for a night on the town, wearing sparkly sequined tops that seemed more Ibiza disco than southwestern dive bar. Tess felt positively plain in her cotton halter and jean skirt.

But at least she wore cowboy boots. She'd bought them the day before she came out. Splurged, to be honest. They were too squeaky stiff to pass muster in a place like this, but she felt more of a kinship with the country crowd than she did with the Lancôme fortified faces before her.

Buffy beckoned Rowdy over and ordered another round of shooters and Long Island Iced Teas.

"And waters all around, please," Tess added. After those wraps, these girls needed H_2O infusions stat, but her earlier pleas for them to go easy on the alcohol had made no impact.

With an eye roll at Tess's mother-hen impression, Buffy barely waited for Rowdy to trip out of earshot before she announced, "Ladies, let's talk dick."

Tess did a ginger ale spit take.

"Buffy, you are too much," Tawny screeched, her eyes bright. "You mean TJ's still got the goods?"

"He might be old, but he's not bad for a guy his age.

Needs a pill, of course, but it all works."

Denise leaned in. Even sitting, she swayed a little, already halfway to getting her drunk on. "Don't it take him forever to get goin'?"

"He's like one of those dial up modems—remember them?" Buffy laughed, the sound grating on Tess's last nerve. "But then once he's got started, it goes to broadband in zero to five seconds. Lightning speed."

"Don't sound very satisfying," Tawny said in a rather smug tone that said she was doing all right in that area herself.

"Oh, he's asleep in two minutes, and then he don't bother me for another month. Next day, I get a nice tennis bracelet or diamond earrings." She looked wistful. "I do okay."

"How's Hunter in the sack?" Tawny asked Tess, a gleam in her eye. "The way he looks at you, like he's hungry as a wolf. Sure is something."

Tess could feel heat rushing to her cheeks, a microcosm of the situation all over her body. The things he had said and done to her, how he had made her feel— It all came back in an erotic flush.

Denise squeezed her hand. "Oh, you two are so in love. It's just wonderful to see."

Swallowing around the lump in her throat, Tess fought for calm, though everything was sliding to shit. To be loved by a man as amazing as Hunter would be wonderful indeed. Just catching mere glimpses of his compassion made her question everything. Earlier, while she made her daytime-TV quality confession, she felt his disgust in her bones at Gavin. When Hunter had offered to hunt that bastard down, she had rejoiced.

There are ways, he'd said. First Derek, now Gavin—

Hunter's protective streak was a mile wide, and boy, did that give her the chills.

She had always thought she was a good judge of character, yet she had screwed up royally when it came to Hunter. But if she hadn't, if she had urged Jenna to go through with the marriage, then Tess wouldn't be here. Pretending to be madly in love with a guy she could see falling madly in love with.

For real.

She had to fight it. It was a classic case of show crush, the affliction that befell actors in close quarters for the run of the show. He was a hot guy with an amazing skill set in the bedroom—the bathroom, the saddle—who aroused the feelings of being loved and protected while he brought on the screaming orgasms. But there was a humongous difference between love and sex. Or love and sex, with a spoonful of compassion and that warm fuzzy feeling of being with a person who could intuit that something was wrong. Who was unafraid to turn over the rock and shine a light on the creepy crawlies of doubt and fear.

No one had tried to get inside her head like that before. That moment when Hunter opened up her body, he unlocked something deeper and unraveled this tight knot of disappointment she had carried for so many years.

Disappointment was an actress's constant companion, but Tess came by it honestly from another source. A wish that her mother could meet her halfway or that Tess was brave enough to demand what she needed. Like she had this weekend with Hunter.

"You know what would be awesome?" she asked the girls, passing over Tawny's request for information about Hunter's prowess. No way did she want to get into a pissing contest with Buffy. "See if we could go ten minutes without talking about a man."

"Well, that'll get boring real quick," Buffy muttered, her eyes wandering to the dance floor. People were lining up rather professionally.

Tess pinned on a smile. "Denise, tell us more about the scary things you've encountered in the dead of the desert night."

"Other than whatever John's hiding in his pants," Tawny added with a smirk.

The girls hooted. Going for more than thirty seconds of man-free talk was apparently too much to hope for.

"It *was* a chupacabra," Denise insisted in a slur. "John wasn't payin' attention to the road."

Tawny rolled her eyes, taking in Tess with an admonishing glance of, *look what you started.* "Come on, Dee. Let's dance off that booze."

They jumped up and wobbled on gravity-mocking heels to the floor, leaving Tess alone with Buffy. A long moment sent the silence from uncomfortable to nipple-freezing awkward.

"So," Buffy said with a shark's smile. "Hunter."

Sipping her ginger ale, Tess considered how best to handle this without pissing off her hostess or forsaking her dignity. "Buffy, I appreciate that you and Hunter have history, but I'd rather not discuss our relationship at this time."

Buffy snorted. "Well, ain't you Miss Snooty? How in the hell did a woman like you land a man like Hunter?"

Truth stings like a mother. *He needed an actress.* All she and Hunter had in common was a hot mutual attraction greased by a smart mouth she wasn't even sure belonged to her. She'd been playing roles so long she had no idea who was the real Tess. Maybe there was no such thing, and she was little more than a procession of wigs and costumes.

"You'd have to ask him. We seem to do for each other all right."

Buffy considered her carefully. "He sure looks at you like you're the cat's pajamas, so you must be doing something right. If it was just sex, he'd have dumped you after a few weeks."

How about in a few hours? The ticking clock in her brain got louder. By tomorrow night, she'd be back in Chicago with a large check, minus a hot fiancé. Sobering in the extreme.

"I guess we understand each other," she fronted.

"Yet, you didn't tell him about your famous mother. Do you know about Alison?"

"I know she was killed by her boyfriend."

Buffy raised a questioning eyebrow, waited a beat, and nodded slowly when she realized Tess had nada. Her gaze skated over the dance floor approvingly where Tawny and Denise were kicking it old school on the line.

"It happened when Hunter was fourteen. He confronted Alison's boyfriend because she was gettin' beat somethin' regular by this guy. He was bigger than Hunter, of course. A real bully with fists to back it up. You know the type." Something close to fear weighed down her eyes.

Tess grabbed the blonde's hand instinctively. "Buffy, you and TJ—"

"Oh, no!" Buffy squeezed back, reassuring Tess that her mind need not go there. "TJ treats me like a queen, but I was with a guy once who showered me with a special kind of affection, you know? I got out, thank God, and a couple years later, I met Hunter while we were working on a charity. Oh, that man could strut sitting down." She smiled, evidently reliving the memory of her first meeting with Hunter. Jealousy-tinged bile rose in Tess's throat.

Sadness crossed Buffy's brow. "He carried the guilt of what happened to his sister with him. He actually thought if he hadn't provoked this guy, his sister would be alive. She was defending him, her baby brother, and this asshole lost it."

Tess's breath froze, momentarily shutting down her lungs. "You mean Hunter was there when it happened?"

"From beginning to end. Half-conscious himself from the beat down. Only reason he lived was because someone heard the commotion and broke into the trailer. By that time, it was too late for Alison. Hunter spent two weeks in the hospital."

Her heart was thudding too fast, her mind racing to keep up. "Why are you telling me this?"

Buffy's shoulders lifted in a negligent shrug. "With no daddy in the picture, Hunter's always thought he should be the one looking after people. His mama, his sister, every woman he's with. But it takes a certain kind of woman to look after him." She sipped on her Long Island Iced Tea. "I'm not sure you're that woman seeing as you hardly know him. You're no more engaged to Hunter Dade than I am."

Bust-ted. Tess's finger flew instantly to twist her fake engagement ring, a gesture that immediately pronounced her as guilty as Hunter's sinful smile.

"He wants that land pretty badly. I guess he needed to impress TJ with his seriousness as a steady guy."

A half smile touched Buffy's lips. "And assure my husband there was no chance Hunter might be sniffing around me. TJ's mighty territorial, I'll tell you." She sounded proud, and Tess registered a twinge of yearning for what TJ and Buffy had, even if it was once-a-month sex with diamonds the next day.

"Why he wants that trailer park," Buffy mused, "I don't know."

"The trailer park?"

"Lindo Pines. Where Hunter grew up, where his sister died, and where his mama still lives. TJ owns it and Hunter is itching to get his hands on it. I expect he's gonna build something on it, but damn, he could do that anywhere. Now, don't you worry about TJ — I'll make sure he sells that property to Hunter." Buffy cocked her head. "Nice story about breaking up his wedding, though. Very creative."

"Oh, that was true. About the only part that is." Along with the fact she was at risk of falling hard for the worst possible guy.

Buffy's smile stretched wide in surprise. "Hon, maybe there's hope for you yet."

"It's just a job, nothing else." Feeble, but that's what she had been reduced to. Weak as a kitten and crazy about a guy who likely still carried a torch for his cheating ex.

Congrats, Tess. You are officially living in a freaking country song.

Buffy looked sympathetic. "Just a job? And I'm a hundred pounds and can still fit in my cheerleader costume. You're in love with that man." She wagged her finger. "You wouldn't be the first."

Forget about being at risk for falling. She was already face planted like a lovesick idiot, and it was obvious for all and sundry to see. Fabulous.

Standing, Buffy gave a catlike stretch, a move that drew plenty of interest from the male patrons propping up the bar. The former Miss Texas still had the goods.

"Now, you ready to learn how to dance country, Tess?"

By the time Hunter made it to the Silver Dollar, he had already tried three bars in Caden, and his mood was as black as the night descending above his head. He should have been back at the ranch, making nice with TJ and losing at cards with the boys, but personal business trumped that. Cecile was MIA, though her broke-down car was not, and Mrs. Hamill said she hadn't been around all day. The guy who owned the diner out on the highway told him he'd fired her a month ago. Only so many times he could put up with her lateness and showing up hungover, or not at all.

Cecile hadn't mentioned that joyful nugget when Hunter came down to clean her up a week ago.

So now his mama was unemployed. Again. All the more reason why he needed to push through his plan and secure her safety. If she spent one more minute at Lindo Pines, she might not make it.

The Silver Dollar had always been one of Cecile's preferred hangouts because she'd had a thing with Harry, the owner, back in the day. The guy knew when to cut her off and make sure she caught a safe ride home. Not that his mother was averse to driving drunk—hell no, she was not—but since she'd had her license suspended and her car knocked out of commission, she had to rely on other folks to cart her around. A lack of wheels did not stop Cecile from having a good time.

The bar was hopping when Hunter pushed through saloon-style doors—a new and touristy touch—and stepped onto the well-worn boards, now vibrating with the dancers' hooves and Kenny Chesney blaring from the speakers.

Fuck, he hated this place. His skin crawled with the fumes, the sawdust, and the scent of violence in the air. In his late teens, he'd enjoyed more fights here than he'd had hot women, looking to use his new muscles to burn off his boiling rage.

He scanned the crowd, lingering a spell on the bar where Cecile would usually be found. No big-haired, bottle blondes snagged his attention. But a gorgeous, petite redhead did.

Miss Tess McKenzie.

Out on the dance floor with the rest of the girls, she was kicking up her boots to the steady tempo, hands on hips, smile breaking wide. Covertly, he watched her awhile, loving how her body undulated with the smooth slide of the line dance. She wore a jean skirt and one of those tops that tied around the neck, and his fingers immediately itched with how easy it would be to unravel it and bare those beautiful breasts to his greedy gaze and touch.

Keeping in step with the line, she looked like she'd been born to the barn, every movement sure and natural. But then she was good at fitting in. Take her anywhere and she figured it out. Chameleon Tess, undercover fiancée.

The music changed to a slower number, Blake Shelton's "Honey Bee," and it was like feeding time at the trough. Every man descended on Tess's group and made a claim, three of them on his woman. She took a couple steps back while the losers jostled and pleaded their case. Primal aggression had Hunter moving in, ready to plead his own.

"Thank you, gentlemen, but I think I'm gonna sit this one out," Tess was saying as he approached. He liked how she stretched out her vowels, playing the part of country girl at the hoe down.

"Maybe I can make you a better offer," he whispered against the shell of her ear, shooting a glare of *back off* at the competition, though he was being mighty generous in his assessment.

It took her a moment to turn, and he knew why. She was composing herself, arranging her expression so she wouldn't look pleased to see him. No matter, her body had already given her away with a sexy shiver as he curled a palm around her shapely hip.

"Why, Hunter Dade, as I live and breathe," she chirped in a spot-on mimic of Buffy.

He enveloped her in his arms and whisked her a few feet away from the covetous eyes of her admirers. The music swirled around them, coating them in good vibes. *You'll be my glass of wine, I'll be your shot of whiskey…* She settled into his body, and the air he breathed was full of her. If it were any more perfect, he'd think it was a setup.

"Cheating on me already, Tess?"

She froze in his arms.

"Hey, only kidding."

Her smile was thin. He stopped and held her hips still. "Somethin' you wanna say?"

Maybe she was seeing someone back in Chicago. He'd asked before he put the proposal to her, and to be honest, he didn't really give her a chance to answer. Hadn't cared. Too busy imagining taking her down a peg while waving those lovely piles of green in front of her face.

The money. It always came back to the money. The only reason a woman as golden as Tess would agree to spend time with a guy like him. Oh, and don't forget his roughneck touch. As if she had an X-ray machine trained on his brain, the next words out of her mouth confirmed what they were both thinking.

"Hunter, about Jenna." Her tongue darted nervously over her lips. "She was… She was all wrong for you."

"Yeah, you've made that clear."

She had the common decency to wince. "No, not because—"

"I ain't talkin' about this now." Jesus H, how many times did he need to be reminded that he was lower than dirt with this woman and her kind?

"Hunter—"

"Tess, I get it." After a long day getting it from all sides— TJ, his MIA mama, his dumb old heart—fury finally frayed his patience. "I didn't even touch her, so don't you worry, Chicago high society was never tainted by our unholy union, not in a church or between the sheets."

Tess's mouth worked to form a response. "Y-you didn't sleep with her. But why?"

"She was so damn perfect," he muttered. Jenna was to be his prize, and you don't get the prize until you've won. Everyone knew that.

Understanding dawned, tingeing her expression with horror. Shit, that had not come out right. Or maybe it had.

"You put her on a pedestal. You wanted to wait until your wedding night."

Not exactly. Part of him was relieved that Jenna didn't seem all that interested, and he convinced himself that the no-premarital-sex decision would make it special later. Putting Jenna on that pedestal implied she was his ideal woman, and sure she had been once—when he had different ideals. He had resigned himself to choosing a wife like a farmer chooses cattle: breeding, weaning, and what it's worth to him in the long run.

Then along came Tess.

A year ago, she had snagged like a burr under his saddle. Sparring with this woman had turned him on, which he was ashamed to admit given that there had been no spark like that with Jenna. Yep, he was a dick squared.

Tess reached out and touched his jaw gently. "That horrible day I know I did the right thing in telling Jenna not to marry you, but I ignored what you were going through, how hurt you were. I hope you find her one day, this perfect woman who can make it all better. Give you that boost you can't seem to get from all you've accomplished. From how far you've come."

She was here. She was *it*.

He wanted to tell her his dreams and hopes and every stinking fear that held him in chains. That she was everything he wanted and the one thing he couldn't have.

Blake was singing his heart out about how he and his girl might be different but they fit each other so right. *If you'll be my soft and sweet, I'll be your strong and steady…* Hunter had thought Tess was out of his reach because she was too cultured, too clever, superior to him in every way, but that wasn't it, or only it. Ultimately, she was so independent that she didn't need his strength. That was all he had to give.

A man like him could never be worthy of even touching a woman like this. But he dared all the same because he wanted to know what it was like to love a goddess, if only for a short while. Hell and damn, he bet those stupid fucking Greeks had a play that fit this scenario to a *T*.

Smooth words or the fancy education to explain what he needed were not in Hunter's wheelhouse. All he had were his hands and the knowledge that when he was inside this woman, he felt like he was home. That, and a few more hours to hold on to it.

"Honey, let's go for a ride."

Chapter Twelve

So that was it, the confirmation she needed that Hunter still harbored feelings for perfect Jenna. So pure that he hadn't even sullied her. Tess couldn't believe Jenna kept that one to herself.

Had she really thought he might want her beyond a few lust-fueled days? Hunter was the man with the plan. Acquisition was the name of the game. Property, a certain kind of woman, respect. She wasn't property, she wasn't a certain kind of woman, and acquiring her for anything more than this weekend wouldn't get him the respect he wanted so badly. She had nothing to offer him but her body.

Wise up, Tess! This was supposed to be a dirty fling to tide her over for a while and help her forget some of her problems. Only now her heart wasn't so sure this was a temporary fix.

Stupid heart.

As she pondered strategies for hardening her love

muscle to this man's assault on all her senses, Hunter spared nothing in his effort to separate them from the bar crowd. They were already halfway through the parking lot, threading their way through a maze of weathered all-terrain vehicles and pickups with gun racks. The cool air whispering across her pantyless ass ushered in reality.

"Hunter, I can't leave. I'm the designated driver."

He pushed her against a car and trailed his fingers down the sides of her thighs, teasing the hem of her skirt up on the return. The stiffness of his erection jolted against her belly.

"Tess, we're not leaving. And don't you worry 'cause I'm designating that you be in control of this ride." His lips hooked up at the corner, a crooked smile that was so sexy and adorable. She was really going to miss him. "I need you now."

The desperation in his voice hit her like a two-by-four. No man had ever broadcast his need for her like Hunter. So it wasn't a need for her like her need for him, but it was honest and earthy. For her own sanity, she just had to act like her heart wasn't full to overflowing when he looked at her with those feral navy eyes.

Acting, schmacting.

"I need you, too." True that. She unsnapped his jeans, watching as his eyes turned hooded and dark with desire. Cupping the hardness between his thighs, she called on her inner sexpot. That greedy bitch didn't have far to travel.

"You make me crazy, Tess, you know that?"

Hunter plucked car keys from his jeans and pressed a button. A click sounded behind her. He yanked open the door of a pickup he must have borrowed from the ranch, one of those older models with a bench seat, and slid into the passenger seat. In two seconds, he had her settled in his lap with her back to his chest. Hot, ragged breaths teased her ear, ratcheting up her desire.

"Hunter, how are we…?" Going to have hot pickup truck sex in this position? She had never done this…any of it.

A shiver cascaded down her spine at the touch of his fingertips to her neck. He undid her halter and pushed down her bra, spilling her breasts free over the strap-free cups.

"You trust me?"

"Yes." Completely, no hesitation. It should have surprised her to even think it, never mind say it with such certainty. But in Hunter's hands she felt safe and secure, especially when the hands were used so well. Those large callused palms dwarfed her ample breasts and roughened her nipples to sharp, painful points.

"Fold your feet up on either side of me and lean forward, Tess."

Stowing away the bothersome notion that *he* had clearly done this before, she placed her hands on the dash, tucked her legs up, and inclined her body to give him the room he needed. This was good. Taking her from behind was hot, but it was also less personal, and she could hide her heart as it beat her unmistakable want in her eyes. Caught between her bone-deep need for this connection and preserving a fragile grip on her sanity, she would gladly take this compromise.

She had no choice.

The hard evidence of his readiness created an irresistibly tempting pressure against her butt. With wanton slowness, she rolled up her skirt and exposed her bare ass. She heard his harsh intake of breath, and the auditory confirmation of what she did to him made her wetter.

"Have you been walkin' around all afternoon like that, Tess?"

"I've been driving around like that and getting my detoxifying seaweed wrap like that and learning to dance country like that."

"You sassin' me?"

She smiled. It did come out a touch impertinent. More wondrous sounds filled the cab. The tear of a condom wrapper, the male grunt as he rolled it on. And then:

Thwack!

What the—? That did *not* just happen.

Hunter Dade slapped her ass!

Indignation demanded she protest but also had the effect of locking her voice up as tight as bark on a tree. The words were still climbing her throat when he did it again, and this time the sting traveled a straight line to her aching clit.

"You remember what I said on my wedding day, Tess? About how the next time I saw you, I'd put you over my knee?"

She moaned, the sound resonating and expanding in the cab of the pickup. Not being able to see him, only hearing his graveled voice was a whole other level of turn-on. He was an exotic stranger who had bundled his captive in his vehicle to have his wicked way with her. But slapping her ass? Surely, her erotic enjoyment of this went against every feminist principle she claimed to have.

Never mind the weird fact he was linking this illicit action to a day they both preferred forgotten.

He palmed her ass, soothing the sting, and...slapped

again. "Remember, Tess? Remember how mad I was?"

"Yes!" This was a thousand kinds of wrong. He was interrogating her about his fucked up wedding day while he spanked her for fucking it up and, mother of God, she was loving every fucking second of it. He massaged her butt cheek and moved his thumb down the cleft of her ass. She lifted off him an inch or two to give him better access and because she needed him there, right there, please, *there*. But he yanked her back and sank two long fingers deep inside her.

Pleasure roared through her, plucking at every last nerve. With a slow, insistent tempo, his fingers pumped her toward ecstasy.

And still he talked about that day. "I was so fucking angry with you." He circled her clit with the fingers he had soaked in her juices and with his other hand squeezed her nipple roughly. So. Damn. Good. Her moans turned high-pitched. Sawing her plump folds against his hand, she grasped the dash for dear life. The thought of how she must look to him, thighs spread wide, rutting on him, spun her pleasure higher toward blistering orgasm.

"I wanted to punish you for interfering." He moved his hand away from her throbbing clit, which right now was the worst punishment she could think of.

Thwack!

Second worst.

"I'm sorry I ruined everything, Hunter." She meant it, every word. She was sorry for her part in it. She was sorry she broke his heart. Now shut up about it and keep doing that thing you do.

"Apology. Not. Accepted." He gripped her waist with

his coarse hands, their skin roughened from building fences and climbing out of the dirt. From becoming the magnificent man he was. With a powerful thrust, he impaled her on his rigid shaft and filled her completely.

Holding her inches above his strong thighs, he fucked her thoroughly from below. Fully in control, his mastery of her blew her away and blew every inhibition out of the water. There would be fingertip-shaped dents in the pickup's dash before they were through, and in her ass from his commanding hold on her flesh.

The quivering of her thigh muscles and the spiraling pleasure in her belly told her that orgasm was imminent. Any second now. It just needed one more— *Ohhh,* he pulled her flush against him and lodged his cock so deep, so tight that she wondered how they could ever part.

She wondered how she could ever want to.

"You see, that day, you set me free," he rasped in her ear.

She moaned. It was all she could do. Moan and feel and listen to what sounded like a strange brew of confession and apology.

"But just for a little while because then you reeled me in when I met you again." He slid out, almost completely, and panic tightened her chest. He was going to leave her hanging in this limbo between pleasure and hell.

He drove into her so hard her vision blurred. She should never have doubted him.

"Now you own me," he growled.

Those words shattered her into a million tiny screams. Mindless with desire, she came with such force her fist lashed out and struck the side window. *Shit, that hurt.*

But she didn't care. Inside her, the man who owned

her heart was branding her with his cock in an explosion of spent desire. His moan of release echoed in the cab of the truck and found a corresponding call back in her still vibrating body. Oh, God. The sound of post-orgasmic bliss and sex-loaded silence was broken by Hunter's groan of repletion. She had done that for him. Not wholesome, up-on-high Jenna. Tess had satisfied his needs.

She sighed, not wanting to move and lose that satiated feeling nor the quiet intimacy she felt while in his strong arms. Those things he said, they clubbed her senseless. He had absolved her of her imagined sin that day, lightened the burden of her guilt.

So much for doggy style being less personal.

Moments later, he let go of a breath and whispered, "You okay, Tess?"

"I don't think I'll ever be okay again. That was…" She reached for words to describe the indescribable. "Almost as good as my detoxifying seaweed wrap."

"Dammit, you want me to spank you again?"

"Yes, please."

He laughed, the rumble of his chest thrilling through her like a joyous choir.

"As much as I'd like to stay inside you all night, I think we need to get ourselves re-situated here."

A few minutes were spent taking care of the necessities, and then they were out of the truck, macking on each other like a couple of hormonal teenagers. The sex had felt different, filled with hope. Forgiveness. Fucked raw by this man in a pickup, and yet, she had never felt more cherished in all her days. He was the first man she had ever trusted, the only one she could imagine holding her safe.

They were both shaking, the moment still profoundly tangible between them. "Tess, my beautiful Tess, I could get used to you," he whispered, the vulnerability in his voice bringing tears to her eyes. "You make me want things that a man like me has no right wanting. There was something about us from the start. Am I wrong?"

No, but it didn't make it right.

"Hunter, I was attracted to you when we first met. It was—"

"Animalistic lust?"

"Incredibly inappropriate. I want to think it had no bearing on my advice to Jenna, but to be honest, I don't know."

He cupped her face with both hands, staring at her, into her soul. "I felt it, too. The bickering, that spark between us. And yeah, it wasn't right, not when I was two ticks away from being a married man."

The guilt on his face killed her. She could say Jenna was cheating on him, burst that perfection bubble he had placed around her. She could alleviate his guilt with a few words but… What would it change? Hunter would still have all the feelings—admittedly confused and unwarranted ones—for Jenna. It wouldn't make him want Tess that way.

Just before he exploded inside her body, he had said Tess set him free that day, that now she owned him. But people said things in the midst of mind-melting bliss all the time.

Didn't they?

She had no idea if this connection was real or just another one of their flash fire bursts of intensity. They both thrived on drama, not exactly conducive to the long-term. At least the sex-with-your-fake-fiancé thing had recognizable boundaries. Now they were entering uncharted waters with a broken GPS.

A horn sounded in the parking lot, and they both jumped and laughed nervously like they'd been caught necking. She needed to say something. Do something. *Anything*. Panic at the thought of losing this opportunity to explore what was happening between them overrode her bone-deep fear of ultimate rejection.

"Hunter, I— I can help you forget her."

He blinked like she had flicked whiskey in his eyes. "Forget who?"

More horns, and now, raised voices punctured the peace. Distracted, Hunter curved his gaze around her in the direction of a couple engaged in a strident argument. His expression curtained to dark.

"I need you to go back inside with the ladies now."

"Why?" She pulled down her jean skirt. Where were her panties? Oh, right. Not wearing any.

"I've got some business to take care of, and I need to make sure you're safe." He slid his phone from his pocket, then dialed as he dragged her by the hand toward the bar.

"Carson, any chance one of you kickers is sober enough to drive?" A couple of beats passed. "Yeah, well, get to the Silver Dollar in Caden, and pick up the ladies. Now." He hung up.

Tess stopped and dug her boot heels in. "You want to tell me what's going on? I'm supposed to drive the girls home."

"I don't like the idea of you hanging out here unescorted. Carson will be here in fifteen minutes, so don't leave before he gets here."

They had reached the entrance to the bar, and the

couple's argument was escalating. Rubberneckers stood off to the side, hoping it would spin out of control in that way people looking for free entertainment had. The woman, a brassy blonde in platform heels, with a low-cut, too-tight dress, was getting all up in the grill of a swaying guy.

"I'm sick and tired of you tomcattin' around," the woman said in a slurry voice like a three-packs-a-day seal. Everything about her was worn, a sepia glow tinting her skin, a recently healed cut marring her lip. Ochre bruises over her eye shone through an unsuccessful attempt to cover it up with makeup. She had to be in her fifties, but the dress was doing her no favors.

Her companion was no catch, either. Pigeon-chested, balding, and with a beer can in his back pocket. How did he sit down without having an unfortunate accident?

"Get inside and wait for Carson, Tess," Hunter said in that stern tone he had when someone was going to get beat. All his attention was riveted to the couple, a muscle ticking like a time bomb in his jaw.

Through the opening above the bar's saloon doors, Tess spied Dee clinging on to the mechanical bull for dear life and… There she went to raucous shouts from the bar patrons.

"If you wasn't such a drugged up whore," Pigeon Chest was saying, "then maybe I wouldn't need to be lookin' elsewhere." And then the prick shoved the woman so hard she toppled over.

All hell broke loose. Hunter grabbed the guy and tossed him against a car like he was a snotty tissue. The look of surprise on his face would have made Tess laugh if she wasn't so worried about Hurricane Hunter inflicting real damage on this guy's face and getting arrested for it.

Tess flew to the aid of the fallen woman who was trying, unsuccessfully, to stand up. She screamed unintelligibly, leaving Tess uncertain if Pigeon Chest or Hunter was her target. Two of the bystanders—and then a third when two wasn't enough—pulled Hunter off before he had a chance to lay complete waste to the guy who liked to knock drunk women over.

"Don't you hurt him!" the woman on the ground screeched. Again, who she was talking to escaped Tess.

Hunter screwed his face up in a grimace. He seemed to be running down a count in his head; then he turned around, shaking off the men who had tried to stop him from going all *Fight Club*.

Squinting up at Hunter, the grounded woman tilted her head. "You never told me you were coming home so soon after last week."

He looked annoyed, but he put it aside to gently pick her up. "I came to see you today, but you weren't home. I've been looking for you all day. Where've you been?"

Oh. Awareness stole up on Tess. This must be…

The woman ignored Hunter's question about her whereabouts and moved her gaze over Tess. "And who've you brung with you?"

"This is Tess. Tess, meet Cecile."

"Your mama," Tess said. *Your mama?* Less than forty-eight hours in Texas and she was talking like she'd been born between two bales of hay.

With a heavy sniff, Hunter's mama swiped at the street dust flouring the tight stretchy material across her butt. She looked over her shoulder, her expression turning as dark as her son's when she laid eyes on the man she had argued with. He was rubbing a hand over his bloodied mouth where Hunter had connected with his fist.

"Hey," Cecile said, pointing a shaky finger. "You'd better watch it. My boy is here, and he could make it so's you'll wish you'd never been born." She took a wonky step, and Hunter checked her with a mild grip on her bare, goosefleshed arm.

"Let's go home, Cecile, before the cops get called out. I've got to leave tomorrow, and we need to talk."

Hunter turned to Tess, his expression troubled. Her heart melted to a gooey puddle.

"Just stay with the ladies until Carson arrives, okay?"

"I'd rather come with you." She had no idea how she would help, but he needed her, even if he didn't quite know it.

"No." He looked inside to where Buffy, Tawny, and Dee were throwing down shots, having moved from the bull to the bar. "You need to keep an eye on them."

Unfortunately, he was right. She nodded, not wanting to pile on to his burden.

The discomfort on his face smoothed to relief. He leaned in and slid his thumb across her lower lip, forcing her eyes shut in pleasure. Quickly, she snapped them open when she recalled she was in public.

There was that shit-eating grin she usually loved, but hated right this minute. The bastard knew exactly how much he got to her.

"Later, Tess."

WELCOME TO LINDO PINES.

The battered sign looked old, maybe from the fifties, unless it was retro. But that would imply some sort of deliberate design choice, and nothing about this place looked deliberate. Barbed wire coils topped the ten-foot high stucco walls on either side of the entrance. The entrance that had no gate or any type of security.

Good thing they had the barbed wire, then.

She'd had a chat with the bartender at the Silver Dollar and got directions to Lindo Pines, about a fifteen-minute drive from town. Once Tony Carson showed up to commandeer her charges, she made her move, but now her heart was a ball of stressed out molecules. What was she doing? Hunter didn't want her here, and there was a good chance she'd get beaten or worse before she could find out where his mother lived. But staying away was not an option.

Butting in was her business and so was Hunter Dade.

A flock of bearded men on folding chairs—the Lindo Pines Welcoming Committee—regarded her with enough interest to warrant a lowering of their beer cans.

Slowing to a halt, she rolled down her window. "Hey, there."

One of them nodded a greeting.

"I'm looking for Cecile." Did she share the same last name as her son? "Hunter's mom."

"She just got home with Hunter," the hairiest one offered. "Drive down to the end and take a right. Her place has geese outside."

"Swans," another chimed in.

"Yeah, swans," the third guy confirmed with a big grin.

"Thanks, guys."

On her slow crawl, she passed dilapidated trailers, some with slide and swing sets out front, chilling reminders that children grew up in this environment. That Hunter had grown up here. She pulled in behind Hunter's truck. A torn awning overhung one side of a single-wide trailer, and a general air of neglect permeated the whole place. Even the plastic swans looked like they wanted to up and fly away. She inhaled a deep breath, preparing herself because she knew he would not be pleased to see her.

The door to the trailer flew open and out stormed Hunter. Definitely not pleased to see her.

Quickly, she scrambled out of their SUV rental so she wouldn't be at a disadvantage. He had more than ten inches on her, but it was better than sitting in leathered luxury.

"What the hell are you doing here?"

"I wanted to make sure you're okay."

"Of course I'm okay. Why wouldn't I be okay?" He sent a stealthy glance over his shoulder. "What about Buffy and the ladies?"

"Tony picked them up. Denise puked on his shoes, so I'm sure he's going to be real pleased when he sees you next." She stroked his forearm, needing the comfort that came from touching him as much as she wanted to give it. "Is your mom all right?"

"Hunter, hon," Cecile called out in a rusty voice. "Is that your sweetheart?"

Hunter closed his eyes, and his long lashes fanned out over the dark circles. He looked so woebegone that Tess wanted to wrap her body around him.

"I'm not here to make it worse. I can help." She stepped in and rubbed his chest with the hand that bore his ring, that signifier of their fake engagement. Yet wearing it seemed to give her a burst of strength. Beneath her fingertips, his heart beat a clamorous tattoo.

"I don't want you here," he said sternly. "It's not your world."

She snaked her arm around his waist. "I'm an actress. They're all my worlds." Her glibness clearly irked him, so she dealt a swift change up to honesty. "But it's yours. This is where you're from, and I want to be here."

"Bring her on in for a drink, hon," Cecile called out. "We're not heathens here."

"If she had any idea what we got up to in that pickup truck earlier, she might revise her opinion," Tess murmured, drawing a half smile from his beautiful mouth.

It quickly faded to serious. "Tess."

As much as she loved her name on his lips, she knew what was coming next would piss her off. She stopped his protest with a kiss, not using sex as a weapon but as a salve. Okay, maybe a combo weapon-salve. After what she had learned about Alison, after all she had seen and heard this weekend, she knew this man needed her right here, right now.

His cool lips warmed as she worked them over, compelling him to relax and surrender.

"You are impossible to resist, Tess McKenzie." Peeved, but resigned.

"Then why bother trying? You know I'm right."

"I refuse to say so because you'll use it against me later. Fuck, here goes nothing," he muttered and led her by the hand to the trailer.

No more than fifteen feet wide, it skewed long and

narrow like a train car. How one person could live here, never mind a mom and two kids, boggled Tess's mind. Empty bottles, take out boxes, and discarded clothes littered every available horizontal surface. Tess could have sworn she saw something move under a pile of clothing in one corner.

In the midst of congratulating herself for striking a balance between polite impassivity and liberal cool, she noticed it. All of it.

Photographs, every inch of wall covered in images of a young girl with Hunter's eyes and a smile that would warm the coldest heart. All ages were represented, from her tomboy beginnings in overalls to when she became more of a girly-girl as her stunning beauty grew in. The entire space paid homage to a beloved dead daughter.

Cecile cleared off a spot on the sofa by throwing more clothes on the floor. She plumped a soft pillow and gestured to Tess to sit. The cushion cover was another photo of Alison.

God, this was just… Tess's eyes flickered in undisguised horror to Hunter. Aloofly, he stood near the door in a stance that combined sentry and imminent departure.

"Sit down and tell me all about how Hunter's doing in Chicago," Cecile said, a tipsy lurch in her voice. "How did you two meet?"

Tess sat, wishing with all her heart that Hunter would sit with her.

"It all happened a while back…" Tess was fairly positive Hunter's mom was not at the wedding, and she had no idea if Hunter had told his mom about Jenna, so she fell back on their invented origin story. "He came to see me in a show and charged backstage after saying he *had* to meet me. It was incredibly romantic."

More lies, more wishes.

She stared at Hunter as she spoke, though his gaze appeared to pass right through her. The chill in that look locked up her lungs. "There was something about him when we met, something I knew would tie me to him. He's an amazing man. You must be so proud."

Cecile gazed at her son, her unfocused eyes welling with pain. "He did it all by himself. I ain't helped him. I ain't helped none of my children." She swiped at her runny nose and took a noisy slurp of her drink.

"Mama, you did fine," Hunter said softly.

"Not by Alison, I didn't." Her hands shook and liquid sloshed over the rim of her lowball glass. "I wasn't around to take care of my baby, to see what she was going through, and now she's dead. Cold in the grave and her mama not there to hold her."

Tess's heart flew out to this poor woman, living with all this guilt. Moving closer, she put an arm around her shoulder. She felt sharp-boned, a bag of antlers poking through skin as thin as wax paper.

"I bet Hunter gets his manners from you. He's such a gentleman, and that comes from upbringing."

Cecile squeezed her hand and gave a watery smile. "Aren't you the sweetest thing?" And then to Hunter, "You gotta keep this one for sure."

Hunter made no response to that, and Tess's heart wrenched.

"Mama, TJ's selling Lindo Pines," he said. "You're gonna have to move. I can find you something nice in Galveston."

Cecile scowled. "There's people lived here for years. My friends. We have bingo every Friday night. And what would

I do in Galveston? What about my job?"

"The one you lost last month?"

Her scowl turned fiercer. "He's always had it in for me. My car wouldn't start—"

"The car you're not supposed to be driving since your license got suspended."

Oppressive silence settled over the small space, soaking into the sagging furniture and crumpled detritus. Mother and son eye-battled it out for long seconds before Cecile dismissed him with a grimace and turned back to Tess. "You want to see a picture of my Alison?"

Apart from the heart-wrenching shrine they were sitting in? Without waiting for an answer, Cecile pulled herself to a shaky stand and reached for a drawer. She yanked on it so hard it tumbled to the floor, its contents spilling everywhere.

"Shit, this whole place is fallin' apart."

Hunkering down, Hunter picked up the strewn papers and knick-knacks. A child's crayon drawings, dented bottle caps, all manner of stuff caught between precious mementoes and useless junk. Cecile snatched something from his hand.

"This one. She's so pretty in this one." She returned to her seat beside Tess, her fingers clutching a photo. "Isn't she pretty?"

Tess took the offered picture. In it, Alison stared out, her gaze a little skewed rather than a full-on stare at the lens. Maybe she had seen something over the shoulder of the picture-taker. Whoever it was had her full attention.

Her thin arms circled the shoulders of a teenage boy, framing him from behind in a protective gesture. It was before Hunter built his muscles, before he started looking up to the stars. But it was there in his navy blue eyes as they held steady for the camera. Determination rang clear across the years.

"She's beautiful," Tess said, her throat scratchy. "And Hunter was so skinny. Not like now."

"Yeah, if he'd had more weight on him then, he might have taken care of business with that bastard who killed my baby instead of gettin' beaten to a pulp."

Shock sliced through Tess at that heartless conclusion, and her eyes shot to Hunter once more. The flicker in his gaze was brief, but he dialed up indifference just as quickly. She knew in her heart it wasn't the first time he'd heard it.

Now Tess realized what was wrong with the images on the walls, in the frames, smothering the small space. Not one of them included Hunter. Jagged edges came into focus in a couple of the framed ones, evidence that someone had been ripped out of the glossy memories. In iconizing her daughter, Hunter's mother had tried to erase her son from existence. It broke Tess's heart. And she thought Deb Patton was a piece of work.

The photo Tess held in her hand couldn't be doctored so easily. Brother and sister were entwined too closely for a simple severance. Surely it meant something that Cecile had kept this. At the very least, it showed she loved her daughter more than she hated her son.

Cecile smiled up at Hunter, a queer grin that chilled Tess to the marrow. "But that Dixon Roberts got his in the end." She took back the photo with a trembling hand, smoothing it out in her lap unnecessarily. "I would have preferred I got my day in court, but wrapping his Chevy around a tree at ninety miles an hour the day after was justice of a kind."

"Cecile, she doesn't need to—"

She held up her hand in defiance.

"Don't you try to shut me up, Hunter Dade. You're always fixin' to shut me up."

"Mama, don't," Hunter said weakly, color forming high on his cheeks.

She grasped Tess's hand and squeezed hard, digging her nails into Tess's palm. Her bloodshot eyes struggled to focus. "Hunter started a fight with that Dixon Roberts. I know he was tryin' to look out for his sister, but Dixon was just too big and mean. And he took it out on my baby girl."

Sixteen years ago it had happened. Tess shut her eyes against the pain in front of her and saw the teenage Hunter, fourteen and scrawny. Now he was as strong as an ox, a knight to any woman who found herself in a vulnerable position.

He was *her* knight.

"Hunter was hurt as well," Tess said, tears stinging her eyelids. In this godforsaken place he had been beaten so badly he was hospitalized for two weeks, and then he came home to a guilt trip so twisted it left Tess reeling. No wonder he wanted out. No wonder he wanted to…

This was the property he so desperately desired, where his mother lived and his sister died. With its purchase, he would make up for his mistake. *Winning is the best therapy.*

Only that wasn't the type of therapy Hunter was going for. This therapy would be deeper and more far-reaching than mere winning. He was going to destroy the park. Obliterate it from existence, and with it, erase the memories of what happened to his sister. What happened to him.

Cecile gave a desultory sniff, her gaze still locked on the photo. "Yeah, he was hurt. But he survived."

And that was it in a nutshell. Hunter was a survivor, and his mother resented him for it. Imagine living with that unrelenting hostility from your own flesh and blood. As for Hunter— She looked up, expecting the same fury she had seen on his face when someone pissed him off.

But not one iota of bitterness marred his rugged handsomeness, and he had plenty of reasons to harbor negativity toward the woman who had given him life. After all these years, his mother still blamed him for what had happened that day, yet Hunter loved her enough to drop everything to come home when she needed him. It humbled Tess to witness it, especially given her inability to forgive her own mother.

Buffy's words reverberated in her skull. *It takes a certain kind of woman to look after him.*

She had no idea if she was that woman, but she knew she'd like to try. Tess had fallen ass over tit for Hunter Dade.

"You know what? I'd love a drink," Tess said, trying to keep the reveal of emotion from her voice.

"Oh, where are my manners?" Cecile made to get up, but Tess stayed her with a hand on her bony shoulder.

"I can take care of it. You visit with Hunter, and I'll freshen up your drink." She took the half-full glass out of her hand, and on rickety legs, headed short strides over to the kitchen counter-slash-bar where she found a cloudy glass and rinsed it out. While she poured and stirred, she listened to Hunter moving around, taking a seat, murmuring unrecognizable words of comfort.

"I can't leave, Hunter," Cecile was saying, her voice breaking like waves on jagged rocks. "This is where she is… It's all I got left of her."

By the time Tess turned back, Cecile was curled into his broad shoulder with her weathered hand clutching that photo like a talisman. Sobs racked her frail, used-up body, still poured into that ridiculous dress.

The sight hit Tess hard.

She was in love with a man who gave her foot rubs and proposed with a ring on her pinky toe. Who "talked" to the director scumbag who made her cry and tracked down odious stepfathers in far-flung lands. Who charged backstage to meet her and annihilated that fortress of distrust around her heart.

So half of those things never happened, but half of them did, and that was enough.

Tess took a sip of her *G & T*. And another.

Then she lowered her love-ravaged body to a nearby armchair, curled her feet up in case anything furry wanted to nibble on her ankles, and watched her man take care of his mama.

Chapter Thirteen

Hunter closed the door to Cecile's bedroom quietly and let go of the breath it felt like he'd been holding all night. The booze and tears had finally caught up with her and dragged her into a deep sleep. Experience told him she'd be out for the night.

What a fucking mess.

He found Tess where he'd left her, looking all wrong and all right in his mama's threadbare armchair. This place should have degraded her, yet she managed to give it a shine of possibility just by sitting there. In the twenty minutes he'd spent soothing his mother to sleep, the trailer had undergone a minor transformation. Laundry and clothes folded, empties disappeared, tidy as a space this small could get.

Something lurched in his chest.

"You didn't have to clean up."

"Will work for *G & T*s," she said with a wave of her empty glass. Her smile crumbled around the edges, and it gutted him how she was trying to put on a good face for his benefit.

She was here, where it all began and ended, not flinching. His brave, beautiful Tess.

Rather than indulging his aching need and dragging her to the sofa, he walked to the sink and leaned against it. If he touched her, he would take her. Indulge every dark desire and selfish want. No doubt about it. He ran his hand through his hair, expecting to come away with the grime of his hated surroundings tattooed to his palms. Shit was always there, in his hair, the cracks of his palms, the folds of his clothes.

She peeked at him through her golden-red lashes, the flicker of awareness at his avoidance of her impossible to miss. "So last week, you dropped everything and came back to help her?"

"It's not as much of a sacrifice as it sounds. One of my business partners, Brody, lets me use his jet when I need it, so I flew down to pick my shitfaced mother up from the drunk tank and took her home."

He had access to a jet. His mother lived in a single-wide. There was irony in there somewhere.

"Not the first time?"

"Not the first time."

She rose to her booted feet and crept toward him, pinning him in place with her serious green gaze. His treacherous body tensed at her approach—dreading, needing, hating, craving. Slender arms wrapped around him. A soft cheek found the pillow of his chest. Breathing was suddenly difficult, but the tightness in his lungs eased up when his arms locked into position, cradling and protecting her. Shit, now he could only breathe right when he held her.

Someone up there despised him.

"Buffy told me the full story about Alison. Your mother's wrong, Hunter. It wasn't your fault. You were just a kid."

The guilt-shaped lump in his chest burned brighter, hotter. He closed his eyes against the million heartbreaking versions of Ali's sunny smile pressing in on him from every angle.

"I knew he was beating on her, but she denied it. Every time. But with each denial, she would shrink into herself like she could become invisible to him. To all of us. And I knew if I didn't do something, he would kill her."

She rubbed his chest, right at that knot of self-hatred, and it flared up again instead of growing smaller. Compassion as kerosene.

"Maybe I should have called the cops, but half the time, they never came and when they did, they'd look at the people who lived here like we were rats. Just vermin that should fight it out, kill each other, and save the taxpayer the trouble. He slapped her one day when she spilled some beer on his jeans. It was so blatant, and I thought if he'd do that in front of me, he'd do worse behind my back. I lost it. Started whaling on him, hoping righteousness was enough to make up for my lack of strength."

Tess raised her head from the perfect spot on his chest and slashed him to pieces with those liquid green eyes.

"Then Ali got involved. She was always defending me because I was weak. This time, I wanted to be the one defending her. But it wasn't enough. I wasn't enough."

"Oh, Hunter, baby," she murmured. "That was not up to you. And now… Well, you can't save everyone, especially the ones that don't want it."

He knew she was talking about Cecile, but she may as well have been talking about every woman he had ever been with, including her. Not that Tess needed saving, but his white knight complex demanded he hold her. Protect her.

Love her.

Yep. Someone up there definitely despised him.

"I owe Cecile for what I took away. She's got no one to fight for her, and yeah, I'm the last person she wants in her corner, but it's me or nothing."

Apparently that was not the right thing to say. A strangled sob hitched in Tess's throat, and she fled his arms and the trailer, leaving in her wake a gust of air completely disproportionate to her petite frame. Following, he found her bent over the hood of the SUV, her shoulders shaking, her fists clenched. A champagne-colored moon cast beams of light over her beautiful hair, spinning it into gold.

"Tess, honey…" He turned her and gathered her close. "I know this is a lot to take in. It's definitely not what you signed on for, and I'm sorry I put you in the middle of it."

Breathing hard, she grasped at a few snatches of air before tipping her head up, her eyes glossy. "You have nothing to be sorry about, Hunter Dade. I chose to come here. I chose to get all up in your business. A year ago. Tonight. I just…" She faded out with a shake of her head.

"You just what?"

"I can't believe how gentle you are with your mom."

Considering how she blamed him for what happened? Not to mention the fact she had made it her mission to delete him from existence like some bizarro version of *It's a Wonderful Life*.

"I'm not a forgiving person, Hunter. I'm judgmental. I

hold grudges. I'm not able to put what happened with my mother behind me, but you, those things she said, what she's done here with the photos... It has to hurt, and still you haven't given up on her. I think that's amazing."

Not once had it occurred to him to give up, though half the time he fooled himself into believing it was the booze that hated him, not his mother. Deep down, he knew her truth came out with the gin, and while his skin would never be thick enough to truly withstand her barbs, blood was blood. He refused to give up on her, no matter what she said or did.

"It's not amazing, Tess. It's stubborn. I see something that needs to be fixed and that's what I do."

In this moment, he was the broken one who needed fixing, but as good as it felt to hold Tess in his arms, he knew it was as ephemeral as the moonbeams in her hair. God, he wanted inside her so badly. Here. Now. And didn't that just say it all? That he was low enough to want to humiliate her in this place. Tonight he had already fucked her like a beast in the truck.

You could take the trash out of the trailer park...

"I'll drive you back to the ranch," he said, releasing her. He had to get her out before he did something that brought them both to ruin. Like screw her blind in a broke-ass trailer park. Lose all sense of time and reason. Fall in love with his fake fiancée.

Too late on that last one, Dade.

"No," she said with a grim determination. "We should stay the night. In case she needs us."

Us. Like they were a team. His heart thundered with an eager, insistently hopeful pulse.

She held his gaze squarely. "Why do you want to buy the land, Hunter?"

"I plan to raze this park and every trailer in it to the ground." Poverty broke his mother, killed his sister, propelled him forward. He had the means now to do anything and be anyone, but not when there was evidence of his roots holding him back.

If she was surprised, she didn't let on. Perhaps these epic plans for revenge and redemption were normal in her world. It did read like something out of a Greek tragedy.

"You think it will help?"

He pretended to consider that for a moment and hoped what came out didn't sound overly rehearsed. "She won't do rehab or let me buy her a new place. A clean break with all the things she uses as a crutch. That's what she needs."

"You think it will help *you*?" she asked, eerily echoing his own thoughts, and then he realized that's what she meant in the first place. Sharp as a tack, his Tess.

"It's not about me," he lied.

She gifted him a skeptical look, calling him out on his shit. He ignored it. He was a fucking pro at ignoring it.

"But what about all the people who live here? Where will they go?"

"I'll help them find homes. The land's too valuable to build low-income housing on it, but I own some property in Caden that would work." In the subsequent quiet, her thoughts echoed loudly in the dark night. "How's it going over there, Miss Judgy?"

"It seems an extreme way of getting one person to do your bidding, Hunter."

"You think people are really happy here?" He waved

around the neglected park, site of his childhood nightmares. "I lived here and I wasn't happy. I'm doing them all a favor."

"Telling people what's good for them never works. They've got to figure it out for themselves."

He growled. "I liked you better when you were playing my compliant, fake fiancée."

"Never compliant, Tex. Just consider this our argument for the day."

"This one ain't up for debate."

She placed her hand on his chest. A shaft of moonlight caught the engagement ring he had given her two days ago, and still it paled in comparison to her. "Hunter, this isn't going to bring back Alison, and it's not going to make your mom any less of a drunk. Instead of healing you, it'll just keep the pain alive, give power to this black thing weighing you down. I know what it's like to hold on to old hurts. It closes you off to the possibilities."

The possibilities? Anger surged to sensitize his skin. At her, at Jenna, at TJ. At every person who told him he couldn't. Well, he could. He had the means, and he could buy this land and a new future for his mother, but he refused to accept the pity in Tess's eyes.

Poor Hunter and his miserable attempt to exorcise those demons.

Poor Hunter was no more. That kid had been left bloodied and beaten on the floor of that trailer sixteen years ago. In the intervening years, he became stronger because only strength could protect, only winning could steal away the hurt. Happiness had always been too abstract for people like him.

At the sharp look he drilled into her, she should have

shrank, but this was Tess, who never backed down from sticking her beautiful nose in when she thought she was right. He knew she didn't approve of his methods, but this was none of her damn business.

Just like getting involved with this woman was none of his.

Tess recognized that look in Hunter's eyes, the one that said she had overstepped her bounds. But she refused to stand down. This plan to erase everything, how would that help? He might think he was doing the right thing and justifying it with his mother's needs, but she saw the bigger picture. His need to atone for what had happened to his sister, as if removing all traces of the event could make it better. Could make him better.

It wouldn't. She had spent years running from confrontation with her mother, and she knew what it was like to suit up your emotional armor instead of facing what's difficult. For years, she had let her bad experiences in her youth and Deb's epic fail as a mom set the tone for every relationship. Trust was forever in short supply. Men came and went.

But not Hunter. He was the most solid man she knew. A tower of strength, a hero for the ages—who still thought he could never be good enough and that cutting through with a broad sweep of power and money would help him make the grade. Homes would be destroyed, and people would be displaced, all in service to Hunter's need to obliterate his painful past. What would it change? His mom would still be an alcoholic, his sister would still be dead. Hunter would still have a hole in his heart.

A hole Tess knew she could fill, if he would let her.

"Hunter, listen to me."

"So you can tell me you know better? No, thanks. You go back to the ranch, princess, and I'll see you tomorrow."

The princess jibe should have clued her in that this would not go well, but still she persisted. "That's it? You won't even listen."

"Your opinion has been noted, but unlike the last time you interfered in my life, you're not goin' to have your way. This plan left the station years ago, and it's runnin' express."

This stubborn man! "Your mom has to want to be helped—"

"Fuck, you don't get it, do you? Look around. This ain't Hollywood. No one here gives two shits about therapy. The medications of choice are drugs, booze, and cold, hard fucking."

"I don't believe that, Hunter. We can talk to her. Together."

He skewered her with an intractable look. "There ain't no *we* here, Tess. There's you. There's me. Employer, employee, and now your job is done."

The words chilled her with their finality. "What about when we go home? Back to Chicago?"

He moved in closer, crowding her against the SUV and caging her with all that brute, male heat. That look in his eye told her something dreadful: *I* am *home, and there's no room for you.*

"You ready for our final argument, Tess?"

Final? "W-what?"

"What was that thing you said last night? About some Russian guy's gun?"

Bafflement left her cold, searching for meaning.

"Chekhov?"

"Yeah, Chekhov's gun. How it's some theater principle that if you show it early, you've got to use it later. That how it goes?"

He cupped her jaw with his strong, callused palm, abrading her skin, roughness and gentleness at once. Across her lower lip, he swiped his thumb, a Hunter move that drove her wild with desire and fear.

"It started in this park years ago. My Act One. And sure I got out for a while, but shit, you never do. Not really." Bending his forehead to hers, he quirked a grim smile. "I'm the gun, Tess. I'm ready to blow, and you don't want to be in the way when I do."

She refused to believe that. He was her protector, the man who owned her heart and restored her shredded faith in the possibility of love. He was as incapable of hurting her as she was of denying that love. If they had a chance, she had to make him see the kick-ass woman who was here, ready to fight for him, just like his sister had done all those years ago.

"I'm not going anywhere. You'll have to physically remove me."

His eyes flew wide at that. Good. Like most men, he needed to be shocked out of his boneheaded idiocy.

"Want me to get rough, Tess? Is that it? Want me to throw you on the hood of this car, ride you hard, make the princess beg?"

No, but she'd happily slam his head against the grille if he didn't quit acting like a jackass. "That's not what I meant and you know it."

"No? Maybe you want another spanking or some more dirty fun in the outdoors?" He leaned in, his breath hot and sweet against her cheek. "You've had your fun, Tess. Your walk on the wild side, your flirt with a bit of rough. We're oil and water, and while everyone loves a little variety, we both know this ain't goin' anywhere. You're not my kind of woman, and I'm not your kind of man."

Liar, liar, man on fire. She tried to take comfort in how the unimpeachable evidence of his arousal against her hip made a mockery of his supposed indifference. She reached up to touch his bristled jaw, and he caught her wrist.

"You think you can pay to make your problems go away, Hunter? Yes, you've got money and power. You can marry a Chicago socialite. You can destroy the historical traces of who you are. It won't change who you are in here." She poked at his chest with her free hand, trying to tell him with her sizzling fingertips who he was at heart. This wonderful, caring man who lit her soul on fire.

"You can't erase the past like you're throwing out a pair of old shoes. It won't get you that acceptance you crave. Only you can give you that. Only you can be the final stamp of approval. No one else."

Not even her.

He closed his eyes, and a surge of victory waved over her. He got it. He understood what she was trying to say.

But when he opened them again, she realized her error. The rampant beast in him was back, the kid with fists too weak to wound, the man with memories too corrosive to forget, and though she knew he would never hurt her, he seemed determined to do an injury to something or someone. Knowing Hunter, the most likely target was himself.

But she was wrong about that as well.

"I ain't lookin' for anyone's approval, Tess. I can buy the

future. Mine, Cecile's. Haven't you heard? Everyone has their price, even a woman as high n' mighty as you." He stared at her, those dark eyes flat and fixed. "You came a lot cheaper than Jenna, though. A hundred thousand. Chump change."

She felt like she'd been struck. He couldn't possibly think that… That she was a commodity for sale. That she was anything like Jenna.

Apparently, not even as good as her. *Cheaper.* She took a step back, tried to, but she was already as far as she could go, wedged against the car.

"Didn't take much convincing, either," he went on. "Didn't take long to have the princess eating out of my hand, or coming all over it. Why'd you think I invited you to Texas, Tess?"

"F-for the job." The job that had turned into so much more.

He barked a mirthless laugh. "Sure, honey, the job. And maybe I wanted to see how low I could bring a woman like you." He threw up both hands. "How you likin' where the weekend has taken you, Tess? You got fucked in a pool house, diddled on a horse, banged in a pickup outside a honky-tonk. The tour bus made stops at an on-the-up ranch and a down-in-the-dregs trailer park, and now you've finished out the evening giftin' us all with your elitist, blue state, big city opinions. We sure are grateful you're here to show us the error of our ways." His growl was filled with dismissive disgust. "Now it's time to toddle back to your city townhouse because your visit to the lower depths is over. Check's in the mail."

He strode off into the trailer, all wounded cowboy swagger, looking as good going as he did coming—even through her blurred, tear-filled vision.

Chapter Fourteen

A few minutes after eight, Tess approached the Escalade parked outside the theater with a Venti extra shot caramel macchiato, and knocked on the window. Just like every night for the last two weeks, the window rolled down to reveal a scary mofo rocking a blond buzz cut, a neck as thick as a bull's, and cat-burglar black.

"Hi, Casey."

"Miss McKenzie."

She handed him the coffee and a packet of raw sugar. He had quite the sweet tooth. "Don't you think it's time the stalker and stalkee were on a mutual first name basis?"

Casey, aka Lurch, the bodyguard assigned to her by one Hunter Dade, gave her a blank look she suspected he practiced in the mirror, and refused to acknowledge her attempt at humor. It was strictly name, rank, and serial number with him.

She let go of a sigh. "I'll probably be leaving earlier

tonight. About eleven thirty."

He nodded curtly, which she translated as, *See you at home.*

Hunter Dade was still protecting her. Forget about shares in Infuriating Asshole, Inc.— He'd taken over as CEO. Each evening, she passed Lurch's car, half expecting to see her starkly beautiful Texan, but he never showed. If she were thinking straight, she'd tell Lurch—and by proxy her ex-fake fiancé—to take a hike. But straight thinking was not in her wheelhouse right now.

Somehow, Hunter had found out where she actually lived, her crappy apartment in her crappy neighborhood. She had come home one night to a new lock to replace the broken one on the front door of her building and a check for her final week at the Bella Sera Playhouse. Plus tips. Hunter's doing, no doubt. There was also the payment for a job well done in Texas, but she had torn it up and sent it back with his ring.

Her living situation maintained this tenuous bond with him, so she stayed put in her dumpy hovel. Let him throw his stupid money around, ensuring her safety. Let him read Lurch's undoubtedly mind-numbing reports about how she spent her day.

Subject returned home at one a.m. after another night painting the walls at her new theater. Paint looks green, but it could be gray in a certain light.

Subject still jawin' on her phone as she walks down a dark, dangerous street.

Subject forgot the extra sugar packets for my damn coffee. Again.

Sighing, she opened the door to her influx storefront

theater and tried to take pleasure in the sight. In two days, they would hold their opening night benefit, and she hadn't needed Hunter Dade's money to do it. Gran had left her an unexpected bequest—twenty thousand dollars—and though it wasn't enough to fund the entire first year, it would start them off right.

No, she didn't need his money, but she needed the man. Her heart was in shreds without him.

"Hello, darling."

Tess spun about to find two-time Oscar winner, Deborah Patton, stepping tentatively inside the theater's entrance. As always, she looked stunning. Ash blond hair perfectly coiffed, subtle makeup that made her look more like an older sister than a mother, and beautifully cut clothes from a designer Tess knew she'd never heard of.

"Mom, what are you doing here?"

"I figured it would be much more fun to spend my birthday with my daughter than with a bunch of nobodies in L.A."

Tess made a ham-with-all-the-fixins meal out of looking around Deb's shoulder. "Is your therapist hiding behind that mailbox?"

Deb laughed, a musical tinkle that was at once nervous and genuine. "When you called last week, you didn't sound like yourself, Tess. I just knew something was wrong with my baby."

Now she could tell? That phone call had been made on the business end of her break-up wallow. Over a fake engagement. Fake or not, it felt entirely real and epically sucktacular as evidenced by two weeks of swollen red eyes, a sofa strewn with snotty tissues, and watching the entirety of Julia Roberts' oeuvre, including her Razzie award nominated performance in *Mary Reilly*. The day she spoke to her mother, Tess thought she had her misery locked down tight, but maybe she wasn't that good an actress, or she was channeling Julia as a downtrodden Irish maid.

"I was going through something, but I'm okay now."

"Boy trouble?"

Man trouble. Heart crushing, soul-destroying man trouble. She supposed for some future role that required her to draw on a past hurt, she might be tempted to use the moment Hunter had dismissed her outside his mother's trailer. More likely, she would focus on that old standby of "dead childhood pet" because reliving even a tenth of the pain she felt right now would leave her doubled over in agony.

Taking Tess's silence for agreement, Deb sighed and cast her gaze around the unfinished space. The crew would be by later for a pre-benefit christening party, but for now, Tess was enjoying the quiet as she moved the furniture around aimlessly, anything to delay returning to her cold Hunterless hovel.

"It's been a long time since I've been in a theater like this."

"A theater this small, you mean?"

Her mom's perfectly lined lips lifted at the corners. "Darling, we all have to start somewhere. Some of my fondest memories are of bombing in theaters this small, then sharing a bottle of indifferent red with the cast while we went through the post-mortem of why the show sucked."

Expectation of bombing? Check. Good old Mom. Always with the little digs. "You never sucked."

"I know, darling. I said the show." She smiled that award-winning smile, and Tess couldn't help returning it. She'd really missed her mother.

"Gran left me some money. I wasn't expecting it, but it was enough to get things started."

Deb nodded. "I never thanked you properly for looking after Mom. You were there when I couldn't be, and I'll never forget it. Whatever she left for you, you deserve it." She shrugged a slender shoulder. "I haven't been the best daughter or mother. I know that."

Tess gulped, uncertain how to frame a response. Was it her job to alleviate her mother of her guilt? Was this going to make Tess feel better?

It might.

Ask for what you need. Words of wisdom from one exasperating Texan who didn't know how to take his own advice. So often the way.

"You didn't stand up for me, Mom. I needed you to protect me and be my shield." Like Hunter had been from the start and without invitation. "Instead, you accused me of stabbing you in the back. It killed me that you would think I'd go after your husband. I was only fifteen. A child."

"I know, darling. Actors aren't always the most sensitive people, despite our job description as vessel." Beautiful teardrops flecked her lower eyelashes like diamonds. "I was in a bad place. Doing that ridiculous witches movie—"

"For which you won a slew of awards."

"There's no accounting for taste, darling. You know that."

Tess managed to suppress an eye roll.

"I thought my career was over, and Gavin had obviously been moving his attentions elsewhere. When you told me what happened, I was so jealous of you. Your youth, your beauty, your talent." She waved an elegant, ring-jeweled hand. "Even when he ran off with that pair of fake tits on a stick, I couldn't get past it until later. And then when I was ready I thought we could move on, get back to what we had."

What they had? Her mother was never around, so getting back to nothing wouldn't have helped much. But bringing all that up now while Deb was trying to make her awkwardly worded peace would be counterproductive. She wanted to move forward, not back.

Start looking up to the stars.

"Mom, I don't know that we can say it's automagically fixed—"

"There's always therapy, darling."

Tess sucked in a fortifying breath. "I'd love if you could listen to me without the intervention of a third party. Just you and me."

Her mother considered that for a few moments. "As long as there's wine and chocolate cake involved, I suppose I can go along with those terms."

More terms. Tess guessed all life was a negotiation, even with the people who were supposed to love you uncondi-tionally. It was always possible her mother didn't have it in her to give that much of herself—not when she owed so much to her art—but Tess didn't want to be the person who looked back on her life and saw she'd treated it like a dress rehearsal. Hunter had shown her that blood matters, and while sometimes people don't need us, it's our need to con-nect with them that defines us.

Right now, Tess was a daughter who needed her mom.

"There's a cute bistro around the corner. I'm sure we can find a table in the back"—she tilted her head in question—

"unless you'd prefer a table at the front."

Her mom's smirk was knowing. "A table at the back will be fine."

As they left the theater, Tess texted Lurch about where she was going. He'd only worry.

At his brusque chin jerk when they walked by the car, her mother raised an eyebrow, no doubt wondering why her daughter was on nodding terms with a man who looked like he should be breaking legs for loan sharks.

"Boy trouble," Tess said. "We might need an extra bottle of indifferent red for this one."

. . .

Four neat pieces.

For what felt like the fiftieth time in the last hour, Hunter studied the precisely torn segments of his check for one hundred thousand dollars. It looked like she had quartered it over the side of a desk or the edge of a book. Maybe the *Complete Works of Shakespeare* or something equally symbolic.

She had also returned the ring, just in case he was too much of a dunderhead to get it.

Your stinking money can't buy me, asshole.

Message received and his head was reeling with it. Not so different from how he had felt in the two weeks since he got back from Texas. With nothing.

Well, that wasn't strictly accurate. He'd come back with a festering case of self-recrimination. He had treated Tess like shit and then pulled his usual stunt. Sent her a nice, fat check for a hundred *K*.

Pain lanced between his eyes, and he called out to the reception suite. "Emma?"

"She's on a coffee run," Flynn said, strutting in like he owned the place. "But only because her boy crush, Mr. Kane, asked." He pronounced his opinion on Brody and Emma with a those-crazy-kids eye roll.

"Saw the courier arrived," he went on when Hunter kept silent. "Did the revised North Shore contract come in?"

Hunter grunted non-committedly and threw the check fragments down, the white contrast against the mahogany of his desk making him wince.

"That's not your happy sound, my friend." Flynn picked up the North Shore documents and took a seat on the sofa. Settled in.

"Any time you want to pass by my office door," Hunter mumbled, "I'd appreciate it."

"You've been more of an asshole than usual lately. You going tell me what happened, or do I have to get Becs on the phone to do my dirty work?"

"Things got problematic."

"Which is a classier way of saying you fucked up." Flynn flicked a glance to the contract for Lindo Pines on the desk. "The actress not going to be nominated for an Oscar, then?"

Hunter gusted a sigh. "Hell, *I* believed we were engaged."

"Yet, she didn't want the money."

She didn't want him, at least not the version who was so hung up on the past he couldn't fathom the possibilities staring him in the face. Tess, sweet, infuriating Tess… She saw into him, cut right through his crap with those sharp eyes and unpalatable conclusions.

He'd run a background check on her, something he

should have done at the start. She had sixteen dollars and forty cents in her checking account. For the last year, she'd been her grandmother's primary caregiver until she passed. And she didn't live in that fancy townhouse with the million-dollar art, but somewhere far more troubling. Past the end of Lake Shore Drive, he had driven until the streets grew less leafy and more asphalt. More dangerous. Turning down her block, he'd quickly registered the grim details: a liquor store on the corner, what looked like a halfway house a few buildings in, sketchy characters huddled in a suspicious group. All in all, a clusterfuck waiting to happen.

Tess's building had seen better days, the poor illumination shedding enough light to enhance the dread pouring through his blood. The gable was in need of repair as was the tuckpointing. A couple of the apartments' windows were boarded up— He'd hoped to Christ that had nothing to do with Tess. Someone had made an attempt to brighten the courtyard with flowers around a non-working, bird-shit streaked fountain, but had forgotten to set up a watering schedule.

She might have had a few preconceptions about him, but he'd had enough about her to fill a four million dollar townhouse.

"We had a fight."

"One of those contractually arranged arguments? Foot rub couldn't do the trick?"

He felt a growl building from somewhere deep. "Nothing can. Like I said, things got problematic."

"On a scale of one to ten?"

Hunter looked up and found Brody leaning in the doorway. *Ker-ist,* throw him through the window behind him now.

"One hundred thousand," Hunter said.

A wince of understanding passed over Brody's face. "So she was looking for more than a walking ATM. Let me guess— You couldn't be what she wanted?"

He couldn't be what *he* wanted. Comfortable enough in his own skin to recognize he'd become a success. That maybe it was time he chiseled away at that chip on his shoulder and enjoyed this good life he had made. Enjoy it with a woman who enjoyed him. He thought back to how amazing Tess had made him feel in so many ways, and not just the sex. When she stood up for him to TJ, when she showed kindness to Cecile, when she melted in his arms like he was the only person who could hold her right.

Flynn looked thoughtful—and worse, concerned. "So what's the problem? You like her, but she doesn't like you?"

Hunter Dade, dumber than boxed soup, had no response for that.

"You *like* like her?" Flynn prompted with an eyebrow raise in case it wasn't clear they were getting into high school gossip territory.

"Jesus, what are we doing? Starting up our knitting circle?"

Brody strode in and sat down on the sofa beside Flynn. The circle was complete.

Looked like there was no getting out of it. His boys wanted to talk. "She's out of my league."

That drew a snort from Flynn that sounded a lot like "Bullshit."

"Did you think Jenna was out of your league?"

"That was different. That was business." He couldn't buy Tess. He didn't want to.

Flynn shook his head. "Marriage as business? I don't get

that at all. You wanted Jenna to put the finishing touch on this life you've created, and that worked out just swell. Do you want whats-her-name for the same reason?"

"Tess," he ground out, torn between irritation that Flynn couldn't recall the name of the woman Hunter was crazy about and embarrassment at his friend's pointed conclusion.

"Why do you want Tess?"

There were a hundred thousand reasons, none of them monetary. Her sly smile, her killer instincts. How she snuggled into him at night. Looking at this woman while she slept in the arms made to protect her, he had lost his breath and thought, *this has to be what happiness feels like.* Because if it wasn't, he never needed to know.

It scared him, how much he wanted to surrender to her request to let go of the past. How much of a hold she had over him. Lashing out at her was supposed to put him back on top in this universe of one, this gloomy place where he used to feel so at home.

But home was in her arms and between her thighs. It was sinking into a sofa at the end of a long day and giving his girl foot rubs. It was ice cream and silly arguments.

He had a lifetime of darkness nipping at his heels, and she was the first flush of dawn. Letting that much light in after so long without it was a risk. He could burn up. He could go blind. Was he prepared to take a chance on this short, intense, forged-in-flames connection?

Every day he made decisions by balancing risk with reward. Here, the risk was his heart, but it was a null and useless thing without this woman in his life. As for the reward? Tess, fighting him. Tess, fighting *for* him.

Just Tess.

Chapter Fifteen

"I can't believe we have an Oscar-winner in the house," Ames muttered out of the side of her mouth.

Tess was having a hard time wrapping her head around it as well. Working the crowd at the theater benefit like a pro, Deb told stories about what so-and-so was like to work with—*an absolute diva, dahling*—and who among the Brat Pack had brought it between the sheets—*rhymes with Bob Toe.*

Embarrassing as hell, but that was her mother.

Tess grabbed a glass from the tray of Cristal toted by one of the white-shirted catering staff her mother had insisted on hiring. *Just my little contribution.*

"She's berating people into making bids on the silent auction." Amy gestured to the long side table parked inside the entrance, littered with prizes such as dinner with Deborah Patton, a spa package from a local salon, and a subscription to the theater's first season. Plenty of other offerings, too, that would hopefully supplement their income for this initial year.

Tommy, their artistic director, walked to the front of the room and tapped the mic.

"Ladies and gentlemen, thanks for coming to this benefit for North Star Theater Productions. We're so excited you could join us on this night where everything begins."

The crowd, mostly friends and family of the company, cheered. Tommy pulled on his bow tie and grinned. He definitely had a *Doctor Who* thing going on. After a special shout out to "our guest of honor, Deborah Patton," and the wait for the applause to die down, he cleared his throat importantly and went on.

"Let's begin the silent auction."

"Beginning" wasn't completely accurate given that the bids had already been made. It was just down to revealing the winners.

As each prize and its winning bid was announced, Tess ran mental calculations. It was going very well, and when dinner with her mother netted a whopping twelve thousand dollars, Tess's heart raised clear through the roof.

Deb lifted a perfectly plucked eyebrow and tried to look gracious. Clearly, she had expected it to go higher, and Tess could hear her now: *Local theater is dead, darling.*

Tess didn't care. She was here, living her dream and doing it her way.

"And now the subscription to the theater's first season," Tommy said, looking down at the sheet in his hand. Below a furrowed brow, he squinted. "Looks like somebody thinks we're operating on the barter system. We're all fans of ice cream and, um, foot rubs here, but that's not going to cut it,

I'm afraid."

Alarm bells rang in Tess's head. *Ice cream? Foot rubs?*

"We'll move back to the last dollar bid," Tommy said, scanning the sheet. "It's six hundred and—"

"Last I checked, this was the United States of America," a graveled voice drawled. "Is my bid not good enough?"

Every hair on the back of Tess's neck stood to attention at that sound. Deep, electrifying, and maddening as all get out. Frantically, she looked around, and her eyes fell on Jenna and Steve—and the towering hulk beside them.

Hunter Dade. God love the man, she would never tire of how well he filled out a pair of jeans. How that could be legal she had no idea.

"Well, sir. Man cannot live on ice cream alone," Tommy intoned, drawing polite laughter from the crowd who got a mild kick out of the play on the literary allusion.

"Perhaps, but I know a woman who could." He locked eyes on her and held it for a terrifyingly sexy number of seconds. "I'll pay eight hundred dollars' worth of ice cream or however much Tess McKenzie can eat in a year, whichever is greater."

"She could eat more than eight hundred dollars," Amy piped up.

"Ya think?" Hunter asked her in all seriousness.

Vehement eyelash batting ensued from her friend. "Oh, definitely."

This was getting out of hand. "Hunter Dade, that's not how a silent auction works," Tess said, trying to keep her voice from shaking as much as her legs, which swayed like reeds. "You don't shout out bids, you're supposed to write it down. It's too late."

His hungry gaze whipped to hers, and she realized that speaking up was like throwing chum in the water. Hunter the predator had her in his sights, but then had she ever really left them?

"No, it's not. I've bid on property and cattle this way. It ain't over till it's over."

For all that good ole boy bravado, Tess would lay odds Hunter Dade had never bought a cow in his life. "Are you comparing me to property…or cattle?"

He moved forward, eating the gap between them with his long, sinuous stride. Eating her up with his dark blue gaze.

"You know my hand spanking your sweet ass is as close to a brand as you're going to get, Tess," he said, sotto voce so only she could hear.

That was… She didn't know what that was, but it sure as hell didn't sound like a denial of her accusation about property or cattle comparisons. The throb between her legs seemed to know, though. It knew Hunter Dade had come to claim his woman.

Whoa, there. She checked that thought to the tune of screeching tires in her befuddled brain. She wasn't a piece of chattel no matter how sexy the outrageous alpha doing the Cro-Mag club-and-drag.

"We've got six hundred dollars here," she called out to a crowd that was more interested in what was playing out between her and Hunter than in the auction itself.

"Six hundred and fifty-six," Tommy corrected.

"What have you got?" she asked Hunter with a calmness belying the heart thundering like a jet engine in her chest.

He took up residence in her personal space and

delivered one of those, *honey, I got what you need* looks. Shallow breaths kept her barely sentient. Relief that he was here, relief that he wanted her, because why else would he do this, floored her.

"I didn't buy Lindo Pines, Tess."

Okay, *that* floored her.

"You were right. It was no way to handle it." He scrubbed a hand through his hair. "Instead I'm gonna use the money to set up a charity. The Alison Foundation. Counseling, education, shelters. Make sure anyone who needs help can get it."

"Hunter, that's just…perfect." Her eyes filled with tears at how far he'd come. Another tilt of his head up to those stars.

"But there's still the matter of you and me, Tess. I could throw a hundred, two hundred thousand, a million dollars at you, and I know it won't satisfy you." He leaned in, smelling incredible, making her dizzy with want. "If I'm to win a woman like you, I really need to bring my *A* game."

She fought a smile. Barely won. "*A*-plus."

"How about an argument?"

"Arguing with you is overrated." *I've missed you so much, you sexy beast.*

"A foot rub?"

Sighing dramatically, she folded her arms, anything to stop her shake. "I've had better."

He smiled, a slow, sultry burn she felt down to her dampening panties. "A year's supply of ice cream…for the whole crew."

A couple of cheers went up from the disloyal brood behind her.

"Now you're just pandering." *Kiss me, you Texas idiot.*

"And a promise."

Every part of her was trembling, wishing like hell he'd take her in his arms and get it over with it. Good God, she was only human.

"A promise?" she choked out.

"To love and protect you as long as I have a single breath in my body."

Oh, mercy. The protection part she understood—it was embedded in this amazing man's DNA—but did he just say *love*? She hoped there was enough in that breath for both of them because her own oxygen supply was dwindling fast. How did he do this to her?

Every. Single. Time.

Passing over the love comment, she pushed forward on the assumption that the mention of it might have been an accident. The kind of thing you say in a moment of passion or weakness or crowd-pleasing at the climax of the rom-com, but regret later. If he meant it, he'd say it again. And again. And again.

"Is that in addition to the ice cream? Because I don't think the crew would forgive—"

He kissed her then, like he was parched after a long day out in the Texas sun. A kiss that dismantled her brain and sent her heart soaring to the stars. When he finally let her up for air, he murmured against her lips, "Why can't you just be quiet sometimes and let me take care of things?"

"I don't know." She really had no clue. "Are we still negotiating?"

"Damn, you're tough. How about a lifetime supply of orgasms?"

"I certainly don't want to share *that* with the crew."

He laughed, a rich and hearty sound. "Orgies are out. Good to know. Mind if we take this somewhere private? I think we've entertained the mob enough for one evening."

Yes, yes, yes. Privacy was what they needed, a place to talk and get things straight…and maybe a few more kisses in between explanations…and Hunter's hands on her breasts and ass and every part of her that felt like it was made for his touch, and his alone.

"Tess?"

"Uh-huh?"

He raised a questioning brow. "Somewhere we can talk?"

She shook her head to clear her sex-addled brain and caught his let-me-do-you grin.

"Oh, there'll be plenty of that. Don't you worry on that score."

Slipping her hand into his felt like comfort food and foot rubs and ice cream, all on her ratty couch with the promise of Hunter-made orgasms later. It felt like coming home. She led him away, but he broke her iron grip.

"Hold on." He leaped up on the stage and took the mic from Tommy. "I want to apologize to everyone for interrupting the evening."

No one in that room looked affronted in any way, not even her mother who was gazing at Hunter with avid female appreciation. *Step off, Mom.*

"Jot me down for $10,000 on that last bid," he said to Tommy.

"Hunter!"

"Don't sass me, Tess. If I have to sit through some Greek

shit on every opening night for the next year, I get to decide how much that's worth to me." He bounded off the stage like a big, sleek cat and grabbed her hand. "Now lead me to heaven, honey."

Hunter warily eyed the room Tess had taken him to behind the stage, assessing it for his needs. Cramped, unfinished, but it had the perfect thing to set the tone and put them straight. A sofa. Well, wasn't that just wild? He pulled her to it and sat her down.

"You need to stay on this side and keep your hands to yourself while we sort this out."

Indignation widened her eyes. "Are you implying I'm the handsy one here?"

He cocked his head, amused when a blush blazed up her cheeks.

"I happen to have needs," she said defensively, crossing her arms beneath her gorgeous breasts. He had missed those pale peachy globes of perfection with that winking freckle and—

Focus, Dade.

Sitting at the other end of the sofa, he said, "I know all about your needs, honey, and I'm gonna take care of them. Gimme your feet."

She toed off her shoes and stretched her legs over his lap, giving him enough hints of creamy thigh beneath her skirt to tide him over for the few minutes he'd need to explain. He had been worried that time away from her would diminish, but it had only enhanced everything: her beauty, his love, the swell in his chest and his cock. They stayed like that for a couple moments, settling into their comfort zone.

"Was that Oscar-winner Deborah Patton I saw out there?"

"It was. We're working things out." Her smile was droll. "And speaking of difficult moms…"

"How long have you got?" He ran a thumb along the arch of Tess's perfect foot, finished off with a purple nail polish, and registered her sexy sound of approval right in his groin. "She's agreed to see a grief counselor, and I'm going to sit in on some of the sessions." Hunter would rather have a root canal with a rusty nail than submit to therapy, but he'd do it for Cecile.

"That's wonderful. A really good step."

"It's not a cure for what ails her, but hopefully she'll start to see there are better ways to deal than drinking herself into unconsciousness."

Brows angled, she asked, "And is she going to move?" *Are you going to make her,* was the unspoken undertone.

He shook his head. Finding other ways to support her would be his focus moving forward. There was no saying how that would go, if she would sober up, if she might learn to forgive him. A lot of fucking ifs. But if he had Tess on his side—sweet, sexy, maddening Tess—he might not feel so alone.

"Hunter…" Worrying her lip, she pinned him to the sofa with a look, both steel and soft at once. "Please can I hold you?"

"I s'pose," he croaked as if he were doing her a favor when really every muscle in his body strained for that longed-for conclusion.

Faster than double-struck lightening, she straddled him and held his face in her hands, searching his eyes for an explanation as to why he'd been so blind and stupid. Why he had pushed her away.

"Tess, I'm sorry for…ah, hell, for everything. All that dumb stuff I said—"

And then she took a page from Hunter Dade's book and kissed away his regrets, letting him know better than any words could that he was an idiot, but he was *her* idiot. Chemical explosions erupted between them as his body caught fire, hardening with every tangle of their tongues. He cupped her world-class ass, cuddled her closer to his cock. This was where she belonged, and he would never let her go.

Breaking away from his searching mouth, she nuzzled his nose and asked, "Why can't you just be quiet sometimes and let me take care of things?"

"Yes, ma'am."

"So respectful. A nice, polite Texas boy." Squirming because he suspected she liked the friction, and undoubtedly because she knew it drove him crazy, she spoke against his lips. "But I know better. I know how raw you want it, how dirty you need it. And you know what else?" She ground hard against him and sucked on his bottom lip. "I know I'm the only one who can give it to you how you like it, Hunter Dade."

"Tess," he breathed. She was right. She did it for him like no other woman. And speaking of other women… He had a bone to pick with her. Shocker. "You should have told me about Jenna, Tess. About what you actually said to her to convince her to jilt me."

She stopped writhing like a sex-crazed pixie and stared at him. "You talked to her?"

"Yup. She came clean about how she was steppin' out

with Puppy-and-Stamps Steve before our wedding day. And you told her that *she* wasn't good enough for *me*."

Her gulp made the narrow column of her swanlike neck bulge. "It just wasn't fair to you, Hunter. What she was doing was all wrong."

Hell yeah it was. Still, no man had ever been so pleased to hear he was being cheated on by his fiancée because the end result was the jackpot: finding out Tess was in his corner from the start and holding her in his arms right now.

"According to Jenna, you said getting married would cause me 'a grave injustice,' which sounds like the kind of thing an actress would say. You told her to quit being a self-ish bitch and to just call it quits."

Color lit high on her cheekbones, and when she spoke, her tone was filled with mild indignation. "Well, she didn't deserve you. I'm pretty sure I mentioned that when we met TJ and Buffy."

When she was acting up a storm? This woman was going to be the death of him, but the ride to hell would be mighty entertaining. "Why didn't you tell me all this before?"

"You made it very clear that you didn't want to talk about your wedding day." A curious vulnerability sparked in her eyes. "And I— I thought you were in love with her. Still."

'Course she did, and true, he hadn't been exactly open to hearing her take on that day's events. The dread at how close he had come to fucking this up shivered through him.

"She's not the only one who was being selfish, honey. I've lived my whole life thinking I'm nothing. I had enough smarts to know I could make a success of myself, but inside, a part of me knew I'd always be on the outside looking in with my nose against the glass. Getting on the other side of that glass consumed me."

"Baby," she admonished with a kiss on his nose.

"I thought marrying Jenna would have given me the respect I needed because it would tell people, it would tell *me*, that I had arrived. I was wrong to use her like that. I didn't love her then, and I wish nothing but happiness for her now."

Her eyes shone bright with emotion, and her breathing picked up.

"You see, Tess, I don't need the respect of strangers or the approval of some club that doesn't want me as a member. All I need is you. And if I have you, then I'll have truly arrived at the place where I'm meant to be and with the woman I'm meant for. I love you. So much. I know it's happened real quick, and I'm probably not what you had in mind for a mate, but damn, no one makes me feel like you do."

Eyes bright and wide, her breath came out uneven. "Say it again."

"I love you, Tess McKenzie." Loud and clear.

Seeming satisfied, she nodded a couple times, and a couple more. "And I…" She inhaled deep and started over. "I'm sorry I interfered at Lindo Pines, Hunter, but I couldn't sit back and watch you do that to yourself."

He swiped his thumb across her fleshy lower lip, trying his damnedest not to be irked that she had yet to tell him how she felt. Maybe he was pushing her too hard. "It's what you do, and yeah, it made me mad, but I need someone like you to put me straight. Tell me how to do things, because I'm going to get it wrong sometimes."

Her face softened in compassion. "We all need someone like that in our lives, Hunter. Someone on our side no matter what."

"So what do you think? Do you want to be the boss of me?"

"You mean officially? Because my unofficial ownership of you has been on the books for some time."

Never a truer word. "Officially. Now and forever."

"Sounds like we need another contract. Where do I sign?" Laughing, she pressed her soft lips to his. "I love you, Hunter."

"Hell and damn, you liked leaving me hanging there, didn't you?"

"Maybe. But more important, I love us."

"We are pretty great," he agreed magnanimously while he got busy moving his hands under her skirt. A silky barrier arrested his progress. *What the—?* "Panties, Tess? You clearly weren't expecting me."

"It's November, I'm a very practical girl, and no, I wasn't expecting you. I hoped so much you might come to see me eventually— And you had your advance scout here, so I felt like you were watching out for me. Casey probably wouldn't appreciate me saying this, but your heart was in that car with him."

Casey would gag if he heard that. "I had to keep an eye on you, Tess. Even if there was no chance for us, I couldn't bear the thought of you without my protection." No matter what happened between them, he would have kept a close watch on her, for the rest of her life, if need be. "And now, I'll take care of you myself. In every way possible."

Slipping his thumbs past the edge of her panties, he found her soft and slick for him. She started up with those sexy little noises of hers, the ones, that along with scorching memories of taking her deep, he had used as alternate sustenance and torture for the last three weeks.

"I want that," she said. "I want you to take care of me. I need it." She kissed him, deepening the connection until his head spun with the possibilities of it all. Of them. "But I'll also be taking care of you."

How had he ever thought he could settle for anything less than this perfect union? Because he hadn't understood that he needed to have someone on his side as much as he needed to protect. A woman like Tess.

He stroked his thumbs through her waiting heat, loving how her rising moans found a rhythm with the throb in his cock and his chest.

Just loving her.

"You're going to make me come," she rasped.

"That's the idea, honey."

She shook her head, fighting him, even on this.

"Inside me, Hunter," she ground out. "That's where I need you. This is a team effort, remember?"

Those words cracked his soul in two and plated it up for her. He undid his pants to free his top player and raised her up a few inches. There was no time to undress, no time for niceties. He just pushed her panties aside and joined his body to hers.

Teamwork at its finest.

She clung to his shoulders, working her tightness over him. The friction of her panties added another layer to their pleasure. Sizzling tension built in his balls, a fierce demand that would need to be obeyed soon. It was happening so quickly, too quickly, and while they might be a team, this was the one race where losing was the best option. His woman would always come first.

In every possible meaning of the word.

He glanced his thumb across her clit, a little roughly because that's how she liked it. She moaned, long and low as her body clenched around him and found her release with the gasp of his name.

Lost in the feel of her, his own release hurtled through him along with the soul-deep knowledge that he had found his way at last. With Tess. They stayed like that for Lord knew how long, taking their sweet time on the ride down where the only thing between them was love and truth.

"That was…"

"Something," she finished on a sated sigh.

"You know what happens now, honey?"

"We have an argument, I get a foot rub, and then we eat ice cream?"

He chuckled. All that and more, but other needs would take priority.

"I think it's time I met your mama. I've got a ring to show her and a question to ask."

She gasped, and that little sound hardened him to mahogany inside her again.

"Told you I was a country boy, Tess. Old-fashioned and used to getting my way. I can't live in sin with you for long, so we're going to have to get hitched. I'm thinkin' something small and elegant. How 'bout it?"

Tears flowed down her cheeks. She kissed him hard and hungrily as she chanted his name over and over like a prayer. Along with one other important word.

Yes.

Yes.

YES.

Epilogue

He could blame the third cup of coffee, but Hunter knew that was not the reason why his stomach felt like it housed a squadron of dive-bombing butterflies.

He pulled at the collar that was doing a fine job of zapping his life force and tried to ignore the fact that everyone was staring at him. His friends. His ex-fiancée and her new husband. His mama and Marta, who gave him a friendly wave. This must be how it felt to be on stage. How Tess did it every night he had no idea.

Then suddenly he lost the fickle crowd as the click-clack of heels belonging to the maid of honor stole their attention.

"Hunter," Amy said on reaching the altar of the intimate Vail Chapel at Northwestern University where he was standing with Flynn at his side. She blew dirty blond curls out of troubled eyes. "Could you come with me?"

He had to be stuck in the recurring nightmare that had been keeping his brain on a stutter for the last month. There could be no other explanation. He looked past Amy to the vestibule. When he didn't see his heart's desire—namely his fiancée making her way toward him with a spring in her step—he swiveled back.

"Where the fuck is she?"

The minister gasped. "Mr. Dade, this is a house of God."

"'Scuse me, reverend, but I have business to attend to, or this will very soon become a house of reckoning."

He took off down the aisle at a brisk pace, acutely conscious of all those judging eyes, every cell in his body primed to detonate because the woman he loved more than anything was not standing at his side getting ready to say, "I do."

In the vestibule, he found Miss Tess McKenzie seated on a bench, a vision in ivory that would have made him hard with lust if he wasn't so rigid with fury. She looked up at him with those soft green eyes.

"Hunt—"

"Are you *tryin'* to kill me, Tess?"

Tess gave a tight smile to Amy, who made a hasty exit through a door off to the side.

"Hunter, I don't think I can walk down that aisle."

Panic scratched at his insides like a bag of rabid raccoons. This could not be happening. Not again.

Standing, she lurched forward, which is when he noticed that she was hopping on one foot. "You know how bad I am on heels. I twisted my ankle getting out of the car and—"

"Honey, sit the hell down." He maneuvered her to the bench and knelt in front of her, feeling for her ankle. Sure thing, it was swelling up something fierce. "You are goin' to an awful lot of trouble to get some Hunter Dade foot rub action."

Looking up, he found her eyes filled with liquid pain. He hated to see her suffering, but his relief that she was *not* jilting him at the altar was coming out ever so slightly ahead. Hey, sue him.

"How much does it hurt, Tess?"

"As long as I don't put weight on it, I'm okay. I think I just need to ice it." She shook her head. "Baby, I'm so happy to be here, and now I'm ruining your big day, the one you've been dreaming of since you were a little girl in Texas." A spark of mischief curled her gorgeous lips.

"Ah, hell, Tess, you ain't ruining my day. You're ruining *our* day."

She laughed. "This is why I love you so much. You always call it like you see it." She looked over his shoulder. "Amy's gone to get an ice pack."

"Amy could have told me what was up before she scared me half to blazes."

Tess's delectably mobile mouth worked, and a twinkle sparkled in her eye. Through her tears, she smiled that sly smile he loved with all his heart.

"You wanted me to have a heart attack, woman."

Leaning down, she cupped his chin and whispered, "I wanted you to be sure. You can still back out, Hunter. Find a girl who doesn't create so much drama or needs to be constantly told how special she is. Your free pass on jilting me is good for the next two minutes."

"Tit for tat, huh?" He cupped one perfectly sculpted breast and stroked it lovingly, pondering the many paths to revenge. "I've got other plans for payback that involve a bed, my tongue, and taking my sweet time making you come." After pulling himself to a stand, he scooped her up and cradled her to his chest where she belonged. "You could be in a full body cast, Tess, and you would still become my wife today."

She giggled against his neck. "For better or for worse…"

"For richer, or poorer…"

"In sickness," she breathed, "and in times when mental health might be suspect."

He stepped into the nave, pleased to see someone had found a chair for Tess at the altar. Amy handed off the bride's bouquet to her with a happily tearful smile, her other hand full with an ice pack.

As he carried the woman who was the center of his world down the aisle to the soundtrack of the "Wedding March" and a murmuring crowd, he whispered his pledge to her.

"I promise to keep it interesting with daily arguments, the kind that'll lead to make-up sex that brings on blushing when you think of it later."

She sighed into him, a sexy feminine sound in her throat that hardened every inch of his body—house of God, notwithstanding. "And I promise to never let you forget that breaking up your last wedding is the best decision I ever made."

She wasn't always right, but she was right about that.

At the top of the aisle, he placed her carefully in the chair and took the ice pack from Amy. After setting it around Tess's ankle, and making sure she was comfortable, he stood and faced the guests.

"Ladies and gentlemen, those of you who have attended a Hunter Dade wedding before will no doubt be unsurprised that things are not going according to plan. And those of you on Tess's side of the aisle will recognize that my fiancée's flair for drama knows no bounds, not even her wedding day. Just one of the many reasons why we are so perfectly matched."

The crowd laughed knowingly. Hunter held Tess's loving gaze, and after affirming with a speaking glance that she was ready for this crazy adventure, he turned back to the minister, a man who looked like his patience was in short supply. Hunter knew the feeling.

"Sorry about that, reverend. Now if you don't mind, I would like to get married to the woman of my dreams today."

And as if Hunter Dade had willed it, the rest of the ceremony went off without a hitch.

Acknowledgments

Thanks to Amber Lin and Nicole Resciniti for reading an early draft and making great suggestions. To über-editor Liz Pelletier for whipping it into shape. And finally, to my source on the world of Chicago theater, Jimmie Meader—thanks for everything you know and all your support.

About the Author

Originally from Ireland, Kate cut her romance reader teeth on Maeve Binchy and Jilly Cooper novels, with some Mills & Boon thrown in for variety. Give her tales about brooding mill owners, oversexed equestrians, and men who can rock an apron or a fire hose, and she is so there. Now based in Chicago, she writes sexy contemporary romance with alpha heroes and strong heroines who can match their men quip for quip.

www.ingramcontent.com/pod-product-compliance
Lightning Source LLC
Chambersburg PA
CBHW020756250626
47155CB00003B/1101